A True Woman of Substance

A WOMAN'S JOURNEY OF SACRIFICE, TRIBULATION AND TRIUMPH

SHIRA MURSALIN BHOGE

Published by:
The 1 and Only Publishing
4500 Forbes Boulevard
Lanham, MD 20706
United States

ISBN (Paperback): 979-8-89741-030-9
ISBN (eBook): 979-8-89741-031-6

Printed in the United States of America.

For information about bulk purchases, author events, or interviews, please contact The 1 and Only Publishing at:
Email: info@the1andonlypublishing.com
Website: www.the1andonlypublishing.com

Cover design: The 1 and Only Publishing
Interior design & formatting: The 1 and Only Publishing

Dedication

To my parents, **Mursalin** and **Jannet**,
whose love and sacrifice shaped my life.

And to my children — **Amarita**, **Serojnie**,
and **Chet Annand** (forever in my heart)
you are my greatest joy and my everlasting inspiration.

Contents

Chapter 1
The Foundation

MORNING ON THE WATER

The rooster's crow pierced the pre-dawn darkness, but Sharifa was already stirring. At twelve years old, she had learned to wake before the call, her body attuned to the rhythm that had shaped her family for generations. The wooden floor was cool beneath her bare feet as she slipped from the small bed she shared with her younger sister, careful not to wake the household.

"Ready, my girl?" her father's voice came softly from the doorway.

Papa stood silhouetted against the faint light, his fishing nets already slung over his broad shoulders. This was their time—just the two of them—before the day exploded into the chaos of farm work, market preparations, and the endless needs of a large family struggling to make ends meet.

Papa wheeled the old bicycle from behind the house, its metal frame worn smooth by years of predawn journeys. Sharifa climbed onto the handlebars, settling herself carefully while gripping the oil lamp that would guide their way through the darkness. The lamp's flame flickered gently as Papa began to pedal, its warm glow casting dancing shadows on the path ahead.

The ride to the water was filled with comfortable silence, the bicycle wheels crunching softly on the dirt road through the village. The air was thick with the scent of blooming frangipani and the earthy smell of the Demerara River. In the distance, Sharifa could hear the soft lowing of their cows, already stirring in anticipation of the morning milking. She held the lamp steady, knowing that this small light was all that stood between them and the darkness that could easily lead them astray.

Out on the water, as Papa cast the nets with practiced precision, Sharifa's mind was already working. She counted the fish as they hauled them in, sorting them by size and calculating what they might fetch at market. Forty-three today—a good catch. The larger ones would go to the hotel in Georgetown, the smaller ones to the local market. She knew exactly which customers would pay premium prices and which would try to haggle them down to nothing.

"You've got the sharpest mind for numbers I've ever seen," Papa said, watching her quick mental calculations. "Even sharper than the men who've been in business for thirty years."

It was a compliment she treasured, though she couldn't yet understand how crucial this skill would become to her survival.

THE SMELL OF INDEPENDENCE

By the time they returned to shore, the sun was painting the sky in shades of coral and gold. At home, their small yard was already bustling with activity. Papa was milking the cows while Sharifa's younger brothers gathered the eggs and fed the chickens. The family's livelihood depended on every pair of hands, no matter how small.

Sharifa's job was to clean the fish—a task that left her hands raw and her school uniform permeated with the smell of the river. She worked quickly and efficiently, her knife movements precise as she prepared each fish for sale. Around her, she could hear her siblings gathering the fruits that had ripened overnight—mangoes, papayas, and coconuts that would join the fish at market.

"Sharifa!" Mama called from across the yard. "Take these to market after school. Mrs. Patterson asked specifically for our mangoes."

At twelve, Sharifa was already trusted to handle sales on her own—a responsibility that would have been unthinkable for most children, but necessity had made her family's children grow up fast. The mathematics came naturally to her, the quick calculations needed to provide correct change, to maximize profit, to ensure the family didn't get cheated by customers who thought a young girl would be easy to take advantage of.

Walking to school with her books balanced on her head and the smell of fish clinging to her uniform, Sharifa held her head high. Some of the other children wrinkled their noses, but she had learned early not to feel shame about the work that fed her family. If anything, she felt proud. While other girls her age were playing with dolls, she was contributing to her family's survival, mastering skills that would serve her for the rest of her life.

THE MATHEMATICS OF SURVIVAL

The one-room schoolhouse was already full when Sharifa arrived, sliding into her seat just as Sister Mary began the morning prayers. School was both an escape and a confirmation of what she already knew about herself—her mind worked differently than other children's, faster and more precisely when it came to numbers.

"Sharifa," Sister Mary called during the mathematics lesson, "can you solve this problem for the class?"

The equation written on the blackboard would have stumped most adults, but Sharifa's mind cut through it like her knife through the morning's catch. The answer came to her instantly, along with two alternative methods of reaching the same conclusion.

"Fifty-seven," she said confidently.

Sister Mary smiled, though there was a hint of concern in her eyes. "Correct, as always. Perhaps you could help some of your classmates who are struggling?"

This was how it started—Sharifa's instinct to help others, to share her knowledge freely. She would lean over to whisper answers to the struggling students, guide them through problems they couldn't solve on their own. She didn't do it for praise or recognition; she did it because knowledge felt like something that should be shared, not hoarded.

After school, instead of playing with friends like other children, Sharifa made her way to the market. Sometimes Mama came with her, but increasingly she was trusted to go alone—a young girl navigating the busy stalls with baskets of produce and fish, conducting business with adults who had decades more experience.

"How much for the mangoes?" a customer would ask.

"Two dollars for three, or seven dollars for ten," Sharifa would reply without hesitation, her mind automatically calculating the bulk discount that would move more product while maintaining their profit margin.

The customer, impressed by her confidence and quick math, would usually take the bulk offer. By day's end, Sharifa's basket would be empty and her pocket would contain the coins that would help feed her family for another day.

THE WEIGHT OF EXPECTATIONS

As evening approached, Sharifa would walk with her grandfather to the mosque for Maghrib prayers. These walks by moonlight were among her most cherished memories—Grandpa's weathered hand gently guiding her along the familiar path, the silver light illuminating their way as they joined other families making the same spiritual journey. The evening prayers grounded her in faith and community, reminding her that even as she excelled with numbers and business, she remained connected to the traditions that had shaped generations of her family.

At home, as the final prayers of the day filled their small house, Sharifa would sit with Papa at the wooden table, helping him calculate the day's earnings and plan for tomorrow's sales. Her younger siblings would be playing in the yard, but Sharifa had been drawn into the serious business of family survival.

"We made eighteen dollars today," Papa would say, spreading the coins across the table.

"Minus three dollars for the boat repair," Sharifa would add, already subtracting in her head. "Leaves us fifteen. If we sell the rest of the papayas tomorrow, that's another six dollars. But we need to save four for next week's seeds."

Papa would nod, marveling at how naturally the numbers came to her. Other fathers relied on their sons to help with business calculations, but Papa had found something even more valuable—a daughter whose mind worked like a perfectly calibrated scale, never missing a detail, never making an error that could cost them money they couldn't afford to lose.

The responsibility was enormous for a twelve-year-old, but Sharifa thrived under it. Every correct calculation, every successful sale, every satisfied customer was proof that she was capable of more than the narrow future most girls in her village could expect. She was building something—skills, confidence, a reputation for reliability that would extend far beyond the borders of their small community.

THE RULES OF FAITH

The strict rules that governed Sharifa's daily life were not just family tradition—they were religious law, interpreted through her Muslim faith and enforced with the kind of vigilance that left no room for deviation. When customers came to buy their produce, if they were young men, Sharifa was not permitted to look directly at them. She would keep her eyes downcast, focusing on the money changing hands, speaking only when necessary to complete the transaction.

"Good afternoon," a young man might say, approaching their stall.

Sharifa would not respond to the greeting. Instead, she would wait for him to state his business—what he wanted to buy, how much he was willing to pay. Only then would she speak, and only about the transaction at hand. No small talk, no eye contact, no acknowledgment of his existence beyond the purely commercial.

At first, this felt natural to Sharifa. These were the rules she had grown up with, as fundamental as breathing or eating. Women were to be modest, protected, separate from the world of men except when business required otherwise. But as she grew older and her mathematical abilities became more apparent, she began to notice how the rules limited her in ways they didn't limit her brothers.

When male customers wanted to negotiate prices, they would often dismiss her and ask to speak with Papa or one of her brothers. They assumed that a young girl, no matter how quick with numbers, couldn't possibly be authorized to make real business decisions. Sharifa would stand silently while the men conducted the exact same transaction she had been prepared to handle, often for less money than she could have negotiated.

But she was learning. Every interaction, every limitation, every small humiliation was teaching her something valuable about the world she lived in and the tools she would need to navigate it successfully.

THE SEED OF AMBITION

It was during these early morning fishing trips and long afternoons at market that the seed of Sharifa's future independence was planted. Not in rebellion against her circumstances, but in the quiet confidence that came from being genuinely, demonstrably capable.

She was twelve years old and already managing significant portions of her family's business. She could calculate profit margins in her head, negotiate with experienced traders, and handle money with the skill of someone twice her age. When customers tried to cheat her—testing whether a young girl would notice if they underpaid or demanded incorrect change—she caught them every time, politely but firmly correcting their "mistakes."

"I think you miscounted," she would say, her voice respectful but unwavering. "The change should be three dollars and fifty cents, not two dollars."

The customer, embarrassed at being caught trying to cheat a child, would usually apologize and provide the correct amount. Word spread quickly through their small community that the young Muslim girl from the cow farm was not someone you could take advantage of, despite her age and gender.

At night, lying in the bed she shared with her sister, Sharifa would sometimes allow herself to dream beyond the boundaries of her current life. She had heard stories of places like Georgetown, where there were proper schools and opportunities for girls who were clever with numbers. She had even heard whispered tales of a place called America, where they said women could work in offices alongside men, where education was valued above all else.

These dreams felt impossibly distant from her reality—a girl who smelled of fish, whose hands were callused from farm work, whose every movement was governed by religious rules that seemed designed to keep her small and contained. But the dreams persisted, fed by every successful transaction, every complex calculation she completed effortlessly, every moment when she proved that her mind was capable of far more than her circumstances suggested.

Sharifa didn't know it yet, but she was already building the foundation of the woman she would become—someone who understood the power of financial independence, who could navigate complex situations while maintaining her dignity, who could see opportunity where others saw only limitation. The girl who would one day save herself and her children was being forged in these early morning hours on the water, in the careful counting of coins at the market, in the quiet confidence that came from knowing she could be trusted with what mattered most.

The cows lowed in the distance, the river whispered its ancient songs, and twelve-year-old Sharifa fell asleep calculating tomorrow's possibilities.

Chapter 2
A World Apart

LEAVING THE FARM BEHIND

At fourteen, Sharifa stood in the yard of the only home she had ever known, watching Papa load her few belongings into the back of a hired cart. The decision had been made—she would live with her older sister Suraiya in town so she could attend Lutheran High School, an opportunity that might never come again for a girl from their circumstances.

The contrast couldn't have been sharper. Where their farm cottage was small and weathered, filled with the constant sounds of cows and chickens, Suraiya's house in the town center was spacious and modern. Suraiya had married well—her husband owned one of the most successful general stores in the region, and their family enjoyed a level of comfort that seemed almost foreign to Sharifa.

"You'll have your own room," Suraiya announced as she showed Sharifa around the house, her voice filled with warmth and genuine affection. "And proper uniforms for school. We can't have people thinking our family can't afford to present you properly."

From the moment Sharifa arrived, it was clear that Suraiya loved her not just as a sister, but like a daughter. The care and attention she lavished on Sharifa was something entirely new—a protective love that came with privileges rather than restrictions.

Sharifa's eyes widened as she took in the polished floors, the electric lights, the kitchen with running water. After years of drawing water from the well and studying by lamplight, this felt like stepping into a fairy tale. The life that awaited her here was nothing short of magical compared to the harsh realities of farm life.

THE FREEDOM OF PRIVILEGE

What surprised Sharifa most was the social freedom that came with living in Suraiya's household, though it came with its own set of rules. Suraiya's husband, Anwar Hoosein, was very strict about regulations regarding boys and boyfriends—these boundaries were non-negotiable. But within those parameters, Sharifa found herself part of a social circle she had never imagined accessing.

"Sharifa, come meet my friends," called Fatima, Suraiya's daughter who was only a year older than Sharifa. "We're going to walk to the ice cream parlor after school."

The children in Suraiya's social circle were affluent, well-dressed, and accustomed to privileges that Sharifa had never dreamed of. Suddenly, she was able to rub noses with these affluent children, to be part of their world in a way that would have been impossible from her farm background.

Walking to an ice cream parlor. Making friends with other girls from prominent families. Having pocket money for small luxuries. These were experiences that felt almost revolutionary after her childhood of dawn fishing trips and market responsibilities.

At Lutheran High School, Sharifa discovered that being Suraiya's sister carried social weight. Other students knew her family owned the prosperous general store. Teachers treated her with a level of respect that seemed to extend beyond her academic abilities. For the first time in her life, she wasn't just the smart girl who helped with numbers—she was someone with connections, someone whose family had influence in the community.

MATHEMATICAL EXCELLENCE

The mathematics at Lutheran High School was more challenging than anything Sharifa had encountered, but her mind seized on the complex problems with the same hunger she had brought to calculating market profits. Algebra, geometry, trigonometry—concepts that left other students bewildered clicked into place for her with almost musical precision.

"Miss Rahman," called Mrs. Patterson during a particularly difficult lesson on compound percentages, "perhaps you could work through this problem for the class?"

Sharifa rose and moved to the blackboard with confidence, breaking down what seemed impossible into clear, logical steps. But what happened next would define her reputation at the school.

Sitting near her was Jennifer, a girl from a family of modest means who was struggling desperately with the mathematics required for her commercial certificate. During examinations, as Jennifer stared helplessly at problems that might as well have been written in a foreign language, Sharifa found she couldn't bear to watch her fail.

Quietly, carefully, she began whispering guidance. Not giving answers outright, but helping Jennifer understand the logic, the patterns, the thinking behind each calculation. Within minutes, other struggling students had leaned closer, creating a small circle of whispered mathematical instruction around Sharifa's desk.

RECOGNITION AND WHISPERS

When the school administration discovered Sharifa's informal tutoring during examinations, what might have been punishment for another student became recognition of an exceptional gift. The headmaster, Mr. Williams, called her to his office not to scold her, but to offer her a formal role.

"Miss Rahman, your mathematical abilities are extraordinary. We'd like you to conduct after-school tutoring sessions for students who are struggling. And when you graduate next year, we'd be honored to offer you a teaching position."

At seventeen, Sharifa became the youngest teacher the school had ever hired. The position came with respect, a steady salary, and status in the community that few young women of any background could achieve. She became quite prominent in the educational circles, known for her innovative teaching methods and remarkable success with struggling students.

But with the recognition came whispers.

"Of course she got the job," she overheard one parent saying at a school function. "Her family owns half the businesses in town. The school can't afford to offend them."

"She's smart enough," another replied, "but let's be honest—without her family's influence, would they really hire someone so young?"

The comments stung because Sharifa knew they diminished her genuine abilities. She had earned her position through mathematical excellence that was undeniable, through a gift for teaching that even experienced educators recognized. But she also understood that in the eyes of many, her success would always be attributed to family connections rather than personal merit.

THE TEACHER'S LIFE

Despite the whispers, Sharifa threw herself into teaching with passion. Her students, many of whom were older than her, quickly learned that her age was irrelevant compared to her ability to make complex concepts accessible.

"Miss Rahman doesn't just give us formulas to memorize," one student told his parents. "She shows us how mathematics works in the real world, how to use it for practical problems."

The teaching position provided Sharifa with something she had never experienced growing up—financial independence combined with social respectability. Her salary allowed her to contribute to her family's welfare while maintaining her own savings. The respect that came with being an educator opened doors that had been closed to the poor farm girl she had been just a few years earlier.

Living with Suraiya's family had shown her what prosperity looked like, what it felt like to move through the world with confidence that came not just from personal ability but from social standing. The contrast with her childhood was stark—she had gone from smelling of fish and worrying about having enough money for basic necessities to wearing proper clothing and being addressed as "Miss Rahman" by community members who sought her expertise.

Her prominence as a young teacher became a source of pride for Suraiya's family, even as some questioned whether her achievements were truly her own or simply the result of family influence.

DREAMS BEYOND THE HORIZON

It was during her third year of teaching that Sharifa first heard detailed stories about opportunities that existed beyond the boundaries of their small community. A former colleague who had emigrated sent letters describing a place called America, where women with mathematical skills could work in banks and offices, where education and ability mattered more than family background or social connections.

"The skills you have, Sharifa," the letter read, "could take you farther than you might imagine. In New York, I have seen women who calculate interest rates and manage accounts for major businesses. They are respected for what they know, not for whom they know."

That night, lying in her comfortable room in Suraiya's house, surrounded by the privileges she had come to appreciate, Sharifa found herself calculating possibilities that extended far beyond teaching mathematics to the children of shopkeepers and farmers. For the first time, she began to imagine a future that was entirely her own creation, built on abilities that no one could question or attribute to family influence.

The seeds of a plan were beginning to form—one that would require strategic thinking, financial preparation, and a kind of courage she was only beginning to understand she possessed.

Chapter 3
Too Big for Small Places

THE RESTLESS TEACHER

By 1969, at twenty years old, Sharifa had outgrown everything that had once seemed sufficient. Three years of teaching at Lutheran High School had brought her respect, financial stability, and a reputation that extended far beyond the boundaries of their small community. Parents from neighboring towns sought her tutoring services for their children. Fellow educators consulted her on mathematical pedagogy. Local business owners asked her to review their accounting practices.

Yet with each passing month, Sharifa felt increasingly confined by the very success she had worked so hard to achieve. Standing before her classroom of eager students, explaining algebraic concepts that came as naturally to her as breathing, she couldn't shake the feeling that she was capable of far more than what Guyana could offer.

"Miss Rahman," her colleague Mrs. Harrison said one afternoon as they walked home from school together, "you seem distracted lately. Is everything alright?"

Sharifa paused, considering how to articulate the restlessness that had been growing inside her like a seed pushing against too-small soil. "Do you ever feel that you're meant for something... bigger?" she asked finally.

Mrs. Harrison laughed gently. "You're already the youngest head mathematics instructor in the region. What could be bigger than that?"

But that was exactly the problem. In Guyana, being the youngest head mathematics instructor was the ceiling, not the floor. The letters from America that continued to arrive painted pictures of possibilities that made her current achievements seem like preparation rather than destination.

Women working as bank managers, calculating interest for major corporations. Female accountants advising business leaders on financial strategy. Universities where women could pursue advanced degrees in mathematics and engineering. A whole world where her gender would be less of a limitation and her abilities could truly be tested.

Standing in Suraiya's comfortable parlor that evening, Sharifa found herself staring out the window toward the harbor, where ships came and went carrying people toward futures she could only imagine. She was twenty years old, financially independent, and intellectually accomplished—but she felt trapped by the very stability she had worked so hard to create.

THE PERSISTENT ADMIRER

It was during this period of restless ambition that Avinash Sharma first appeared outside Suraiya's house. Sharifa noticed him immediately—not because she found him attractive, but because his presence was so persistent and obvious that it became impossible to ignore.

"There's that young man again," Fatima observed one afternoon, peering through the lace curtains. "He's been standing there for over an hour."

Sharifa glanced briefly in his direction, taking in his well-pressed clothes and the gold watch that caught the afternoon light. He was pleasant-looking enough, she supposed, but something about his presumptuous gaze irritated her. She was twenty years old and had never been permitted to have conversations with young men, let alone romantic relationships. The idea of marriage felt abstract and unwelcome—an interruption to ambitions that were finally taking shape.

"He works on ships," Suraiya mentioned casually over dinner. "Travels between Georgetown and New York regularly. They say he's done quite well for himself in America."

The word America caught Sharifa's attention, though she kept her expression neutral. Ship work meant steady income and, more importantly, legal residency in the country that had begun to occupy so many of her thoughts.

But when she looked at Avinash Sharma, standing day after day outside their house with his patient determination, she felt only annoyance. She had spent years building her independence, establishing her professional reputation, saving her money. The last thing she wanted was to surrender that autonomy to a man whose primary qualification seemed to be his willingness to loiter on street corners.

"What does he want?" she asked Suraiya one evening, after spotting him through the window yet again.

"I think his intentions are quite serious," Suraiya replied carefully. "He's asked about your family, your education. He's thinking of marriage."

The words settled over the room like dust, heavy and unwelcome. Marriage had always been inevitable—a social obligation that would eventually demand her attention. But Sharifa had imagined it would come later, after she had achieved more of the goals that drove her restless ambition.

THE FIRST PROPOSAL

When Avinash Sharma finally approached Anwar with a formal marriage proposal, the conversation took place in the family store while Sharifa waited at home, pacing the parlor like a caged animal. She had no say in the initial negotiations—such decisions were made by men, for women, according to traditions that seemed increasingly outdated to someone who had spent years managing her own financial affairs.

"He seems respectable," Anwar reported later. "Good income from his shipping work, established residence in New York. He's offering to provide for you completely—passage to America, housing, everything you would need to start a new life."

The mention of America sent a jolt through Sharifa's chest, but it was quickly followed by resentment. The opportunity she had dreamed of was being offered as part of a package deal that would require surrendering everything she had built for herself.

"And what does he expect in return?" Sharifa asked, though she already knew the answer.

"A wife. A traditional wife who will manage his household and bear his children."

The description felt like a cage door slamming shut. After years of intellectual independence and professional respect, she was being asked to become someone's dependent, someone's domestic manager, someone whose identity would be entirely subsumed into the role of Mrs. Sharma.

When she was finally permitted to meet with Avinash directly—always under careful supervision, always with family members present—Sharifa studied him with analytical precision. He was polite enough, clearly successful in his endeavors, and obviously sincere in his intentions. But she felt no spark of attraction, no emotional connection that might justify the enormous sacrifice marriage would require.

"Miss Rahman," he said during one of their chaperoned conversations, "I understand you're an educator. I respect that. In America, there are opportunities for women with your abilities."

"What kind of opportunities?" she asked, genuinely curious despite her reservations.

"Schools, businesses, banks—they all need people who are good with numbers. And they don't care about your background, just your abilities."

The promise was appealing, but Sharifa couldn't ignore the fundamental inequality of their arrangement. He would be gaining a wife and domestic partner. She would be giving up her career, her independence, her entire life as she had built it.

After three meetings, she made her decision.

"I'm not ready for marriage," she told Anwar firmly. "I appreciate Mr. Sharma's interest, but I must decline his proposal."

THE DEPARTURE

Avinash Sharma received the rejection with more grace than Sharifa had expected. There was disappointment in his eyes, certainly, but also a kind of resigned understanding that suggested he had been prepared for this possibility.

"I hope you'll reconsider someday," he said during their final supervised conversation. "America really would offer you opportunities that don't exist here."

"Perhaps," Sharifa replied politely, though privately she doubted she would change her mind. "I wish you well in your endeavors."

Within a month, Avinash had departed for New York, and Sharifa returned to her teaching routine with relief. She had preserved her independence, maintained her professional status, and avoided what felt like an unfavorable exchange of her current achievements for uncertain future possibilities.

But as the months passed, the restlessness that had driven her initial ambitions continued to grow. Her salary, while adequate for her current lifestyle, would never be sufficient to fund independent emigration to America. The opportunities available to her in Guyana, while respectable, felt increasingly limited compared to the possibilities she read about in letters from colleagues who had emigrated.

Standing before her classroom of students, explaining mathematical concepts she could have taught in her sleep, Sharifa found herself wondering if she had been too quick to dismiss Avinash Sharma's proposal. Not because she had developed any romantic feelings toward him—she had barely thought of him since his departure—but because he represented access to the larger world her ambitions demanded.

GROWING AMBITIONS

By early 1971, two years after Avinash's departure, Sharifa's dissatisfaction with her circumstances had crystallized into a clear understanding of what she wanted: access to opportunities that matched her abilities, regardless of the personal cost required to obtain them.

The letters from America had continued to arrive, each one painting pictures of a society that valued education and competence above traditional social restrictions. Women working as accountants for major corporations. Female mathematicians pursuing advanced degrees at universities. Business owners who succeeded based on their skills rather than their family connections.

Most tantalizing of all were the stories of financial independence that went far beyond anything possible in Guyana. Salaries that would allow for comfortable living, savings that could fund further education, professional recognition that opened doors to advancement rather than merely maintaining status quo.

"I've saved nearly everything I've earned for three years," Sharifa told Suraiya one evening, spreading her carefully accumulated money across the kitchen table. "But it's still not enough for passage to America, let alone establishing myself there."

"You could continue teaching here," Suraiya suggested, though her voice lacked conviction. "You've built a good life."

"A limited life," Sharifa corrected. "I'm twenty-two years old, and I can already see the boundaries of what's possible for me here. In ten years, twenty years, I'll still be teaching the same students, solving the same problems, earning the same respect that goes nowhere."

The mathematical precision that had always guided her thinking was now applied to the equation of her own future. In Guyana, she could maintain her current comfortable existence indefinitely, but advancement beyond her present position was virtually impossible. In America, she would face uncertainty and challenge, but also access to opportunities that could transform not just her own life but potentially the lives of any children she might have.

The variable that could change the entire equation was access—specifically, legal access to American opportunities. And there was only one pathway to such access that remained available to her.

As she lay in bed that night, calculating possibilities and weighing options with the same analytical approach she brought to mathematical problems, Sharifa found herself wondering if Avinash Sharma might return to Guyana. And if he did, whether his offer might still be available.

Chapter 4
The Ticket to America

THE RETURN

In the spring of 1972, Avinash Sharma returned to Guyana after nearly two years in America. Sharifa first learned of his arrival not from seeing him, but from the familiar network of community gossip that carried news faster than the postal service.

"That young man who was interested in you—he's back," Fatima mentioned casually while they prepared dinner. "Mrs. Patel saw him at the market yesterday. Says he looks more prosperous than ever."

Sharifa's hands stilled on the vegetables she was chopping, though she kept her expression neutral. Two years had passed since she had rejected his marriage proposal, two years during which her restlessness had grown into a consuming desire for opportunities that seemed increasingly impossible to achieve through her own efforts.

"I suppose he'll be visiting family," she replied evenly, as if the news held no particular significance for her.

But that night, lying in her comfortable bed in Suraiya's house, Sharifa found herself calculating the possibilities that Avinash's return might represent. She was now twenty-three years old, still unmarried in a society where most women her age were already managing households and raising children. Her teaching position, while respectable, had become as confining as it was secure. The money she had saved over five years, while substantial by local standards, remained insufficient for the kind of independent emigration that would give her access to the American opportunities she craved.

Three days later, he appeared outside Suraiya's house again, taking up the same patient vigil that had characterized his courtship years earlier. But this time, when Sharifa glanced through the window and saw him standing across the street, she didn't feel the same irritation she had experienced before.

This time, she saw possibility.

THE STRATEGIC ASSESSMENT

"He's asked to speak with you again," Suraiya informed her one evening, her voice carefully neutral. "Through proper channels, of course. He wants to renew his marriage proposal."

Sharifa nodded, her mind already working through the calculations that had become second nature to her. In the two years since his departure, her circumstances had remained essentially static while her ambitions had continued to grow. She was older now, more aware of the limitations that constrained her future in Guyana, and more realistic about the sacrifices that might be necessary to transcend those limitations.

"What do you think?" Suraiya asked, studying her sister's face.

"I think," Sharifa said slowly, "that opportunities like this don't present themselves often."

It was not a romantic answer, but it was an honest one. Avinash Sharma represented something she could not achieve on her own: legal access to America, financial security during the transition to a new country, and immediate resolution to the social pressures that surrounded unmarried women of her age.

When they met again—in Suraiya's parlor, under the same careful supervision that had characterized their previous encounters—Sharifa studied Avinash with different eyes. He was pleasant enough, clearly successful, and obviously sincere in his intentions. More importantly, he was offering her passage to the life she had dreamed of for years.

"Miss Rahman," he said, his voice respectful but hopeful, "I hope the time that has passed has given you opportunity to reconsider my proposal."

"It has," she replied truthfully. "Tell me about your life in America. What opportunities exist there for someone with my background?"

His face brightened as he described the world he had inhabited for the past two years. Jobs in accounting firms that valued mathematical precision. Banks that hired women as clerks and tellers, with possibilities for advancement based on performance rather than family connections. Evening courses at colleges where women could study business and finance. A society where education was respected regardless of gender or background.

"And you believe I could access these opportunities?" Sharifa asked.

"Absolutely. Your mathematical abilities, your teaching experience— these are exactly what American employers value. You wouldn't be starting over; you'd be building on what you've already achieved."

For the first time since she had known him, Sharifa felt something approaching interest in Avinash Sharma. Not romantic interest—she still felt no emotional attraction to him whatsoever—but the kind of strategic interest she might feel toward any arrangement that could advance her goals.

THE HONEST CALCULATION

That evening, alone in her room, Sharifa forced herself to confront the reality of what she was considering. She did not love Avinash Sharma. She barely liked him as a person. Their conversations were pleasant enough, but she felt no spark of connection, no desire for his company beyond its practical utility.

What she felt was something else entirely: recognition that he represented her best—perhaps her only—pathway to the life she had imagined for herself.

"I want to go to America," she said aloud to her empty room, testing how the words sounded. "He is my ticket to America."

The phrase felt both liberating and unsettling. She had always been honest in her calculations, whether they involved market prices or family finances. This would simply be another kind of calculation, with higher stakes and more complex variables.

Marriage to Avinash would mean:

- Immediate access to American residency
- Financial security during her transition to a new country
- Freedom from the social pressures of remaining unmarried
- Opportunity to pursue the professional advancement she craved

The cost would be:

- Surrendering her independence to a man she did not love
- Converting from Islam to Hinduism, against her family's wishes
- Leaving behind the life she had built in Guyana
- Accepting a relationship based on strategy rather than affection

When she performed the calculation with the same analytical precision she brought to mathematical problems, the answer seemed clear. The benefits outweighed the costs, particularly when she considered that the alternative was remaining trapped in circumstances that, while comfortable, offered no pathway to the larger life she envisioned.

Three days later, she informed Suraiya of her decision.

"I'll accept his proposal," she said quietly.

"Are you certain?" Suraiya asked, searching her sister's face for any sign of romantic feeling.

"I'm certain that this is my opportunity," Sharifa replied, echoing the words she had spoken years earlier about her teaching position. "I may not get another one."

THE FAMILY STORM

The decision to accept Avinash's proposal created immediate tension within Sharifa's extended family. The religious implications of marrying a Hindu man were serious enough, but the broader questions about her motivations sparked conversations that ranged from concerned to hostile.

"You're the second one to marry outside the faith," her aunt said during a particularly difficult family gathering. "Do you understand what this means for our reputation in the community?"

"I understand what it means for my future," Sharifa replied, though she could feel the weight of disapproval settling around her like smoke.

Her parents, while supportive of her desire for a better life, struggled with the religious conversion that marriage to Avinash would require. Her younger siblings looked at her with confusion, unable to understand how their successful sister could choose to abandon so much for a man they barely knew.

"But do you love him?" her youngest sister asked one evening, the question innocent but piercing.

Sharifa paused, considering how much honesty the moment required. "I respect him," she said finally. "And I believe we can build a good life together."

It was not a lie, but it was not the whole truth either. The whole truth was that she did not like Avinash Sharma at all. He seemed pleasant enough, but something about his presumptuous confidence irritated her. When he looked at her, she could see that he believed he was offering her a gift—the chance to become his wife, to be provided for, to be taken care of.

What he could not see was that she was offering him a gift as well: herself, her abilities, her potential for contributing to their shared success. The difference was that he saw marriage as her salvation, while she saw it as their mutual opportunity.

THE ENGAGEMENT

The formal engagement ceremony took place in Suraiya's parlor, surrounded by family members whose expressions ranged from supportive to concerned to openly disapproving. Sharifa wore her best dress and accepted Avinash's ring with appropriate grace, though privately she felt as if she were signing a business contract rather than celebrating a romantic milestone.

"You'll need time to learn Hindu customs before we marry," Avinash mentioned during one of their chaperoned conversations. "I want you to be comfortable with the ceremonies and traditions."

"Of course," Sharifa agreed, though her voice carried a careful neutrality. "I'll learn what I need to participate appropriately."

"And the conversion process—"

"I'll participate in your family's ceremonies," Sharifa interrupted gently but firmly. "But I need you to understand that my faith is not something I can simply change. I am Muslim, and I will remain Muslim."

Avinash's expression shifted, revealing the first real tension of their engagement. "But our children—they'll need to understand Hindu traditions, be part of the community—"

"They can learn about both traditions," Sharifa replied. "But I cannot pretend to believe something I don't believe. I hope you can respect that."

The conversation revealed a fundamental difference in their expectations that neither had fully addressed during courtship. Avinash had assumed that marriage would naturally lead to her adoption of his faith and customs. Sharifa had agreed to participate in his traditions while never intending to abandon her own spiritual identity.

"I see," he said finally, though his tone suggested the matter was far from settled. "We'll... work it out."

The engagement period passed in a blur of preparations that felt both exciting and increasingly tense. Immigration paperwork had to be completed, wedding arrangements had to be made, and Sharifa had to begin the process of learning Hindu rituals she could perform without believing. Her few possessions needed to be packed for shipment, while she prepared herself psychologically for a transformation that went far beyond changing her address.

Most challenging of all was navigating the growing tension between her family's expectations and Avinash's assumptions about her religious flexibility. She had agreed to marry him and participate in his family's traditions, but she had never agreed to stop being Muslim.

The engagement period passed in a blur of preparations that felt both exciting and terrifying. Immigration paperwork had to be completed, wedding arrangements had to be made, and Sharifa had to begin the process of dismantling the life she had built in Guyana. Her teaching position would need to be filled, her savings would need to be converted to American currency, and her few possessions would need to be packed for shipment.

Most challenging of all, she had to prepare herself psychologically for a transformation that went far beyond changing her address. She was about to become Mrs. Avinash Sharma, wife and dependent, trading her hard-won independence for access to opportunities that might or might not materialize once she reached America.

THE HONEST MOMENT

Two weeks before the wedding, as Sharifa sat in her room packing her few belongings, Suraiya knocked softly on her door.

"May I come in?"

"Of course."

Suraiya settled onto the bed beside her, studying the neat piles of clothing and books that represented five years of independent adult life.

"Are you happy?" she asked quietly.

Sharifa paused in her packing, considering the question. Happy was not the word she would have chosen to describe her emotional state. Determined, perhaps. Hopeful. Occasionally terrified. But happy?

"I'm satisfied that I'm making the right choice," she said finally.

"That's not what I asked."

For a long moment, the sisters sat in silence. Finally, Sharifa spoke with the honesty that had always characterized their relationship.

"I don't love him, Suraiya. I don't even particularly like him. But he is my path to America, and America is my path to the life I want. If that makes me calculating rather than romantic, then so be it."

Suraiya nodded slowly. "And you think you can build a marriage on that foundation?"

"I think I can build a life on that foundation. The marriage will be what we make of it."

It was the most honest assessment Sharifa had made of her situation, and saying it aloud brought her a measure of peace. She was not betraying her principles by marrying without love; she was honoring her deeper principle of taking responsibility for creating the life she wanted.

The girl who had learned to count fish by lamplight was about to become a woman who would cross an ocean in pursuit of dreams too large for the small world trying to contain them. Whether those dreams would prove achievable remained to be seen, but Sharifa Rahman was prepared to find out.

Chapter 5
Crossing Waters

THE WEDDING CEREMONIES

Three days before the Hindu wedding, Sharifa insisted on the Nikah ceremony. In Suraiya's parlor, surrounded by her Muslim family members, she sat beside the imam with a sense of profound relief. This ceremony was hers—authentic, meaningful, rooted in the faith that had shaped her entire life.

"Do you, Sharifa Rahman, accept Avinash Sharma as your husband according to Islamic law?" the imam asked in Arabic, then repeated in English.

"I accept," Sharifa replied, her voice strong and clear. This acceptance carried weight that the upcoming Hindu ceremony never could. Here, she was not performing rituals she didn't understand or believe—she was making a commitment within her own spiritual tradition.

Avinash sat respectfully nearby, though she could sense his discomfort with the Arabic prayers and Islamic customs he didn't understand. But this had been her condition—that their marriage would honor both traditions, not just his.

The Nikah was simple and solemn—the signing of the marriage

contract, prayers for their union, and blessings from her Muslim family. For Sharifa, this was her real wedding, the ceremony that mattered to her heart and soul. Everything that followed would be performance for the sake of social harmony.

The Hindu ceremony three days later took place in the courtyard of Avinash's family temple. Standing in the elaborate red sari, Sharifa felt like an actress in an elaborate play. She had spent months memorizing the words and movements, but she performed them as learned behaviors rather than expressions of faith.

The rituals were complex and beautiful—walking seven times around the sacred fire while Avinash held her hand, speaking Sanskrit vows she had memorized phonetically. As the ceremony concluded with final prayers and the tying of the mangalsutra around her neck, Sharifa felt the weight of her transformation from independent woman to married wife. The priest blessed their union with traditional Sanskrit words, and the gathered families offered their congratulations and well-wishes for their journey to America. The scent of incense and ceremonial drums filled the air while relatives offered blessings for their future.

But even as she participated in every ritual, Sharifa's heart remained with the prayers she had spoken three days earlier in Arabic, the faith that connected her to generations of her ancestors, the spiritual identity that marriage could not and would not change.

"Mrs. Sharma," Avinash said quietly as they accepted congratulations from the wedding guests, trying out her new legal name.

"Different," she replied honestly, though she managed a small smile. "But I suppose I'll get used to it."

What she didn't say was that while she would answer to Mrs. Sharma in public, in her heart she remained Sharifa Rahman, Muslim woman, daughter of her faith. The Hindu ceremony had made their marriage legal and socially acceptable, but it had not transformed her spiritual identity.

The reception was filled with congratulations and well-wishes, but Sharifa moved through it knowing that the real foundation of their marriage—the Nikah ceremony—had been built on her terms, within her faith.

Sharifa moved through the celebrations with practiced grace, accepting well-wishes from people who saw her as either very fortunate or very foolish, depending on their perspective on marriages that crossed religious and cultural boundaries. Whatever challenges lay ahead in America, she would face them as a Muslim woman who had made strategic compromises for practical reasons, not as someone who had abandoned her deepest beliefs for the sake of social acceptance.

"You look beautiful," Fatima whispered as they stood together during a quiet moment between ceremonial obligations. "Are you nervous about leaving?"

"Terrified," Sharifa admitted. "But also excited. This is what I've worked toward for years."

"And Avinash? Are you happy with him?"

Sharifa glanced across the courtyard at her new husband, who was deep in conversation with several older men about shipping routes and business opportunities in New York. He looked prosperous and confident, exactly the kind of man who could provide the stability and access she needed to build her American life.

"He's a good man," she said carefully. "We'll make it work."

THE JOURNEY

The airplane that carried them from Georgetown to New York three weeks later was Sharifa's first experience with air travel, and the four-hour flight felt both terrifyingly fast and impossibly slow as it carried her away from everything she had ever known.

Pressed against the small window during takeoff, watching the familiar coastline of Guyana shrink beneath them until it disappeared entirely, Sharifa felt the magnitude of what she had chosen settling around her like a heavy cloak. There was no turning back now—her teaching position had been filled, her few possessions were packed in

their luggage, and her legal status had been transformed from independent woman to dependent wife.

"Second thoughts?" Avinash asked, noticing her grip on the arm-
rest as they climbed through the clouds.

"More like twentieth thoughts," Sharifa replied with dry honesty
that surprised a laugh out of him.

"That's understandable. You're leaving behind everything familiar
for something completely unknown."

"We both are," she pointed out. "You've been living alone in
America. Now you have a wife to consider."

Avinash nodded thoughtfully. "I've been thinking about that. I
want you to know that I don't expect you to simply... disappear into
domestic life. Your mathematical abilities, your teaching experience—
those are assets that shouldn't be wasted."

The comment surprised her. During their courtship, he had spoken generally about opportunities for women in America, but she
had assumed that once they were married, he would expect her to
focus primarily on household management and child-rearing.

"What do you mean?" she asked.

"I mean that once you're settled and comfortable with English—
American English, which is different from what we learned in
school—you should look into continuing your career. Teaching, or
accounting, or whatever appeals to you most."

For the first time since accepting his proposal, Sharifa felt a genuine warmth toward her new husband. The possibility of maintaining
her professional identity had been one of her deepest concerns about
marriage, and his unprompted support for her career ambitions suggested a flexibility she had not expected.

"You wouldn't mind having a working wife?" she asked.

"I'd mind having a wife who was unhappy because she wasn't using
her abilities," he replied. "We'll both do better if we're both contributing to our success."

34

MANHATTAN ARRIVAL

New York City in July 1972 was an assault on every sense Sharifa possessed. The heat rose from concrete sidewalks in waves that made the humid air shimmer like water. The noise was constant and overwhelming—car horns, construction sounds, voices speaking in languages she couldn't identify, music spilling from open windows and storefronts. The buildings rose impossibly high above streets that seemed barely wide enough to contain the flow of traffic and pedestrians that moved with urgent purpose she didn't understand.

"It's a lot," Avinash acknowledged as their taxi wove through traffic toward their Manhattan apartment. "But you'll get used to it faster than you think."

Their first home as a married couple was a tiny one-bedroom apartment on the fourth floor of a walk-up building on the Lower East Side. The space was smaller than any room in Suraiya's comfortable house, with a kitchenette that barely deserved the name and a bathroom down the hall that they shared with three other families.

"It's temporary," Avinash assured her as she stood in the middle of the main room, taking in the narrow bed, the single window that looked out onto a brick wall, and the small table that would serve as both dining surface and workspace. "We'll save money here for a year, then move somewhere with more space."

"It's fine," Sharifa said, though privately she wondered if she had made a terrible mistake. After years of comfortable living in Suraiya's spacious house, this felt like moving backward rather than forward.

But as the days passed, she began to understand the apartment's advantages. The location put them within walking distance of several banks and accounting firms where Avinash had contacts. The neighborhood was full of immigrants from various countries, which meant their accents and unfamiliarity with American customs made them blend in rather than stand out. Most importantly, the low rent meant they could save nearly half of Avinash's income for their planned move to Brooklyn.

ADJUSTMENT AND DISCOVERY

The first months of marriage were marked by a cautious politeness that gradually warmed into something approaching partnership. Avinash was attentive without being overwhelming, helpful without being condescending, and patient with Sharifa's adjustment to both American life and married life.

"The key to American business," he explained during one of their evening conversations, "is networking. People need to know who you are and what you can do before they'll trust you with opportunities."

He introduced her to his contacts in the shipping industry, to other Caribbean immigrants who had established themselves in various professions, and to the managers at local banks who were always looking for people with strong mathematical skills.

"Mrs. Sharma has a background in education," he would say, his pride in her accomplishments evident. "She was the youngest mathematics instructor at her school in Guyana. Exceptional abilities with numbers and teaching."

The introductions led to part-time work helping other immigrants with tax preparation and bookkeeping, which provided both income and insight into how American business operated. Sharifa discovered that her mathematical skills were indeed in demand, and that her careful approach to financial management was especially appreciated by small business owners who had been burned by less meticulous accountants.

More surprisingly, she found herself genuinely enjoying her husband's company. Away from the formal structure of their courtship and the pressure of family expectations, Avinash revealed a sense of humor she hadn't suspected, a genuine interest in her thoughts and opinions, and a thoughtfulness that manifested in small but meaningful ways.

He would bring her flowers from street vendors, not because it was expected, but because he noticed she missed the garden at Suraiya's house. He encouraged her to maintain correspondence with her family, even though international postage was expensive. Most importantly, he treated her intelligence as an asset to their partnership rather than a threat to his authority.

"You see patterns in numbers that I never notice," he admitted one evening as they reviewed their budget and savings goals. "I'm good at making money, but you're better at managing it."

GROWING AFFECTION

Six months into their marriage, as they celebrated their first American Christmas in their tiny apartment, Sharifa realized that something unexpected had happened. She had begun to care for Avinash Sharma in ways that had nothing to do with his utility as a pathway to American opportunities.

It wasn't the passionate love of romantic stories, but something steadier and more practical—a deep appreciation for his kindness, respect for his competence, and genuine enjoyment of their shared goals and conversations. When he returned from his shipping runs, she found herself looking forward to his company rather than simply tolerating his presence.

"I think I'm starting to like being married," she confided to Suraiya during one of their expensive long-distance phone calls.

"You sound surprised," Suraiya replied, amusement evident in her voice.

"I am surprised. I expected marriage to feel like... a constraint. But Avinash treats me more like a partner than a dependent."

"And how do you feel about him?"

Sharifa paused, considering the question that went to the heart of her transformation. "I respect him. I enjoy his company. I trust his judgment, and I think he trusts mine. If that's not love, it's at least the foundation for love."

The conversation marked a turning point in how Sharifa thought about her marriage. She had approached it as a strategic arrangement, but it was evolving into something much more substantial—a genuine partnership between two people who complemented each other's strengths and compensated for each other's limitations.

PLANNING FOR BROOKLYN

As their first anniversary approached, Avinash and Sharifa began planning their move to Brooklyn. They had saved enough money to afford a proper one-bedroom apartment in a neighborhood with tree-lined streets and access to better schools—important considerations as they had begun discussing the possibility of children.

"Bed-Stuy has a growing Caribbean community," Avinash explained as they studied maps and rental listings. "Good connections to Manhattan for work, but more space and lower cost of living than staying in the city."

"And after Brooklyn?" Sharifa asked.

"Queens, eventually. Better schools, more stability for raising a family. By then we should have enough saved for a down payment on a small house."

The progression he outlined—Manhattan to Brooklyn to Queens, each move representing a step up in their circumstances—appealed to Sharifa's systematic approach to life planning. They were building something together, creating a foundation that would support not just their immediate needs but their long-term ambitions.

More importantly, she was beginning to trust that Avinash's vision for their future aligned with her own goals rather than constraining them. He wanted her to succeed, wanted their partnership to thrive, wanted their eventual children to have opportunities that neither of them had possessed growing up.

As they packed their few possessions for the move to Brooklyn, Sharifa reflected on the unexpected turn her life had taken. She had married Avinash Sharma as a means to an end, but their marriage was becoming an end in itself—valuable not just for what it provided access to, but for what it was creating between them.

The girl who had learned to count fish by lamplight was becoming a woman who could count on her partner's support as they built their American dream together, one carefully calculated step at a time.

Chapter 6
Learning to Love

BROOKLYN BEGINNINGS

The apartment in Bedford-Stuyvesant was a revelation after the cramped quarters of their Manhattan walk-up. Two bedrooms, a proper kitchen with full-sized appliances, and windows that actually let in natural light transformed Sharifa's daily experience of married life. For the first time since arriving in America, she had space to think, to plan, and to imagine a future that extended beyond mere survival.

"Now this feels like a home," she said as they arranged their modest furniture in the main room, already envisioning how the space might accommodate the family they had begun discussing.

Avinash smiled, clearly pleased with her reaction. "Wait until you see the neighborhood. There's a library two blocks away, a park where you can sit and read, and enough Caribbean families that you won't feel like such a stranger."

He was right about the community. Within weeks of moving to Brooklyn, Sharifa found herself part of an informal network of immigrant women who shared resources, advice, and the challenges of adapting to American life while maintaining connections to their home cultures. The conversations reminded her of the market gossip from her childhood, but with higher stakes and more complex problems.

"The key," explained Mrs. Thompson, a Jamaican woman who had been in Brooklyn for five years, "is to become American enough to succeed, but not so American that you lose yourself."

It was advice that resonated with Sharifa's own approach to her marriage. She was learning to be Avinash's wife without losing her identity as an independent, intellectually capable woman. The balance required constant negotiation, but it was becoming easier as she realized that Avinash genuinely wanted her to maintain her individuality.

PROFESSIONAL GROWTH

With more space and a better location, Sharifa was able to expand her bookkeeping services beyond simple tax preparation. Word spread through the Caribbean community about the young woman who could untangle complex financial records and explain American business regulations in terms that made sense to people who had learned different systems in their home countries.

"Mrs. Sharma has a gift for making numbers tell stories," one client told another, leading to referrals that kept Sharifa busy three days a week while still allowing her time to adjust to her new country and marriage.

The work was satisfying in ways that went beyond financial contribution. Each client she helped establish better financial records was building toward the American dream that had drawn them all across the ocean. Every small business she helped navigate tax obligations or banking relationships was contributing to the broader success of their immigrant community.

More importantly, the professional recognition was helping Sharifa see herself as more than just Avinash's wife or an immigrant struggling to adapt. She was becoming Mrs. Sharma, small business consultant, trusted advisor, woman with her own reputation and expertise.

"You're building something important," Avinash observed one evening as they reviewed her growing client list. "People trust you because you understand both where they came from and where they're trying to go."

"Is that why you married me?" Sharifa asked, half-joking but curious about his answer.

"I married you because you were the smartest woman I'd ever met," he replied without hesitation. "Everything else—your beauty, your adaptability, your strength—those were bonuses."

UNEXPECTED INTIMACY

Nine months into their Brooklyn life, Sharifa realized that what she felt for Avinash Sharma had evolved far beyond strategic appreciation. She looked forward to his returns from shipping runs not just because of the income or security he provided, but because she genuinely missed his company, his conversation, his presence in their shared space.

The transformation had been so gradual that she couldn't pinpoint when respect had become affection, when partnership had become intimacy, when practical cooperation had become something that felt remarkably like love.

"You can grow to love someone," she told herself during one of Avinash's week-long absences, acknowledging a truth she had been slow to recognize. "It doesn't have to start with passion. It can start with respect and patience and shared goals, and grow into something stronger."

When she shared this realization with Suraiya during one of their weekly phone calls, her sister's response was knowing laughter.

"I was wondering when you'd figure that out," Suraiya said. "Your letters have been sounding less like business reports and more like love letters for months."

"Have they?" Sharifa asked, genuinely surprised.

"'Avinash helped me negotiate a better rate with the landlord.' 'Avinash brought me books from the library.' 'Avinash thinks I should consider taking college courses.' You write about him the way I write about my children—with pride and affection and the assumption that everyone else finds him as interesting as you do."

The observation made Sharifa laugh, but it also prompted deeper reflection about the nature of the relationship she was building. She had entered marriage expecting to tolerate her husband while pursuing her own goals. Instead, she was discovering that her goals were becoming their goals, and that Avinash's success felt as important to her as her own.

FAMILY PLANNING

The conversation about children began naturally, emerging from their discussions about the second bedroom in their Brooklyn apartment and their plans for eventually moving to Queens.

"Good schools are expensive," Avinash mentioned as they walked through a neighborhood they were considering for their next move. "But they're an investment in our children's futures."

"How many children are we planning?" Sharifa asked, realizing they had begun discussing their hypothetical family as a certainty rather than a possibility.

"Two, maybe three. Enough for them to have siblings, but not so many that we can't provide well for each of them."

The practical approach to family planning appealed to Sharifa's systematic nature, but she was also beginning to imagine the emotional dimensions of parenthood. Children who would carry both their cultures, who would have opportunities neither parent had possessed, who would represent the ultimate success of their American experiment.

"I'd like our children to know both their heritages," she said. "Hindu traditions from your family, Islamic values from mine, and American opportunities for both."

"That's a lot of complexity for children to navigate," Avinash observed.

"We're navigating it," Sharifa pointed out. "They'll learn from our example."

RELIGIOUS ACCOMMODATION

The religious differences that had caused such tension during their engagement were being resolved through practice rather than theory. Sharifa participated in Hindu observances that were important to Avinash, while he respected her private Islamic prayers and dietary preferences when they didn't conflict with social obligations.

"I don't expect you to abandon your faith," he told her during one of their discussions about raising children. "But I do hope our children will be comfortable with both traditions."

"They will be," Sharifa assured him. "Children are adaptable. They'll take what serves them from both backgrounds and create something that's uniquely their own."

The compromise was working better than either of them had expected. Sharifa found elements of Hindu philosophy that complemented rather than contradicted her Islamic beliefs, while Avinash discovered that her commitment to her own faith deepened rather than threatened her commitment to their marriage.

Most importantly, their religious differences were teaching them both about the kind of flexibility and mutual respect that would be essential for raising children who would need to navigate multiple cultural expectations.

GROWING SUCCESS

By their second anniversary, Avinash and Sharifa had achieved a level of financial stability that exceeded their initial projections. His consistent work on shipping routes, combined with her growing bookkeeping practice, had allowed them to save enough money for a down payment on a small house in Queens while still maintaining an emergency fund that provided security during uncertain times.

"We're ready for the next step," Avinash announced one evening, showing Sharifa listings for houses in neighborhoods with good schools and established Caribbean communities.

"Queens," Sharifa said, looking at the photographs of modest but well-maintained homes with small yards and proximity to transportation. "Our final destination."

"For now," Avinash agreed. "Once we have children and they're established in school, we'll stay put. Stability is more important than constantly upgrading."

The decision represented more than just another move—it was a commitment to putting down permanent roots, to building the kind of life that could support children and grandchildren, to becoming not just American residents but American citizens with a stake in their community's long-term success.

REFLECTION ON LOVE

As they packed their belongings for the move to Queens, Sharifa found herself amazed by the transformation their marriage had undergone. She had agreed to marry Avinash Sharma as a strategic decision, a means of accessing opportunities she couldn't reach on her own. Two years later, she could honestly say she loved her husband—not with the dramatic passion of romance novels, but with something deeper and more reliable.

"I fell in love with him," she would later tell people who asked about their arranged marriage, "because he was very good to me and very nice. You can marry someone you like and you can love him. You can fall in love with that person. It can happen."

The love she felt for Avinash was built on respect, shared goals, daily kindnesses, and the gradual recognition that he genuinely wanted her to succeed and be happy. It was love built on the foundation of partnership rather than infatuation, and it felt more durable because of that foundation.

Standing in their Brooklyn apartment for the last time, looking at the space where she had learned to be a wife and discovered she could be a wife without losing herself, Sharifa felt profound gratitude for the unexpected gift her strategic marriage had become.

She had crossed an ocean in search of opportunity and had found not just professional advancement but personal fulfillment. The girl who had counted fish by lamplight was now a woman who had learned to count on love, partnership, and the possibility that the best decisions sometimes led to destinations more wonderful than anything she had originally dared to imagine.

As they loaded their possessions into the moving truck that would carry them to Queens and the next phase of their American dream, Sharifa took Avinash's hand with genuine affection and anticipation for whatever came next.

Chapter 7
The Good Years

The house in Queens felt like a promise fulfilled. Three bedrooms, a small backyard where children could play, and enough space for the family Sharifa had begun to dream of. As she stood in the empty living room that first day, sunlight streaming through the windows, she felt something she hadn't experienced since leaving Guyana—hope taking root.

"This is it," Avinash said, setting down a box marked 'Kitchen.' "Our real beginning."

For once, Sharifa agreed with him completely.

The move from Brooklyn had been Avinash's idea, but Sharifa had embraced it wholeheartedly. The apartment had served its purpose, giving them a foothold in America and a place to fall in love. But a growing family needed more space, more permanence, more of the suburban dream they had both carried from their childhoods in Guyana.

"Remember your father's house?" Avinash asked one evening as they unpacked dishes in their new kitchen. "How proud he was of those fruit trees in the yard?"

"He spent every weekend tending to them," Sharifa replied, smiling at the memory. "Mango, coconut, breadfruit. He said a man wasn't truly settled until he had trees that would outlive him."

"Well, we've got an apple tree," Avinash said, gesturing toward the small backyard. "And room to plant more. Maybe some day our children will pick fruit from trees we planted."

The thought filled Sharifa with unexpected emotion. For the first time since leaving home, she could imagine creating something lasting, something that would grow and flourish long after they were gone.

The first years in Queens unfolded like the pages of a storybook she might have read as a child, if such books had existed about ordinary people finding extraordinary happiness. Avinash had found steady work at a manufacturing company, his engineering background from Georgetown finally put to good use. The supervisor, an older Jamaican man named Mr. Williams, had taken an immediate liking to Avinash.

"Good to have another Caribbean man on the team," Mr. Williams had said during Avinash's first week. "These Americans, they don't understand our work ethic."

The camaraderie among the Caribbean immigrants at the plant created a sense of community that Sharifa hadn't expected. Wives would gather for Sunday dinners, sharing recipes that reminded them all of home. Children played together while parents talked politics and reminisced about the countries they'd left behind.

"It's like having family again," Sharifa told Avinash after one particularly lively gathering at the Williams' house.

"Better than family," he replied. "We chose each other."

Sharifa discovered she was pregnant just three months after they moved in. The morning sickness that had eluded her during their apartment days hit with vengeance in the new house, sending her rushing to the bathroom each morning before Avinash left for work.

"Maybe it's the change in water," she said weakly one morning, her head resting against the cool bathroom tile.

"Maybe it's something else," Avinash said gently, his hand rubbing circles on her back. "When was your last monthly?"

The realization hit them both at the same time, and suddenly Avinash was whooping with joy, picking Sharifa up and spinning her around the bathroom despite her protests about her queasy stomach.

"A Queens baby," he kept saying, his hand on her still-flat belly. "Born in America, just like we planned."

"Born in America, raised with love," Sharifa added, already imagining the child who would grow up truly belonging to this country in ways she and Avinash never quite would.

The pregnancy progressed smoothly once the morning sickness subsided. Avinash became almost comically protective, insisting on carrying groceries and forbidding Sharifa from cleaning the windows or reaching for anything on high shelves.

"You act like I'm made of glass," she protested one afternoon when he rushed to help her up from the couch.

"You're carrying precious cargo," he replied solemnly. "The most precious cargo in the world."

Their neighbor, Mrs. Kowalski, a Polish immigrant who had raised six children in the house next door, became an unofficial pregnancy advisor. She would lean over the fence between their yards, offering unsolicited advice about everything from nutrition to nursery setup.

"First baby always the hardest," she declared one sunny afternoon. "But also the most special. You never love like you love that first baby."

"Did you love the others less?" Sharifa asked, genuinely curious.

"Not less," Mrs. Kowalski said thoughtfully. "Different. Each baby teaches you something new about love. First one teaches you that you can love someone more than yourself. Others teach you that the heart just keeps growing."

Saira arrived on a crisp October morning in 1972, screaming her way into the world with a ferocity that made the nurses laugh. "She knows what she wants," one said, placing the baby in Sharifa's arms. Looking down at her daughter's perfect face—tiny features that somehow combined the best of both parents—Sharifa felt her heart expand in ways she hadn't known were possible.

"She has your determination," Avinash whispered, kissing Sharifa's forehead. His eyes were bright with tears he wasn't ashamed to show. "And my stubborn streak."

"God help us all," Sharifa replied, but she was smiling.

Avinash proved to be a natural father from the very beginning. Where many new fathers seemed bewildered by the tiny, fragile creature they'd helped create, Avinash approached fatherhood with the same methodical care he brought to his engineering work. He read books about child development, practiced diaper changes on a doll Mrs. Kowalski had loaned them, and learned to prepare bottles with the precision of a chemist.

"You're going to spoil her," Sharifa said one evening, finding Avinash sitting in the nursery rocking chair, reading aloud from a book of poetry to their three-week-old daughter.

"Impossible," he replied without looking up. "You can't spoil a baby with love and attention. Besides, she likes Wordsworth. See how still she gets when I read about daffodils?"

Those early days with Saira were a blur of feedings and diaper changes, of learning to be a mother while still learning to be an American. But Avinash surprised her daily with his devotion. He would come home from work and immediately reach for the baby, walking her around the house while Sharifa prepared dinner.

"In Georgetown, my father never held us," he said one evening, Saira sleeping against his chest. "He thought it wasn't manly. But we're not in Georgetown anymore."

"No," Sharifa agreed, watching her husband's gentle hands support their daughter's head. "We're Americans now. American fathers love their children openly."

The community of Caribbean immigrants embraced their growing family. Sunday dinners at various houses became extended affairs, with multiple generations sharing stories and traditions. Saira would be passed from lap to lap, absorbing the rhythms of Guyanese speech and the warmth of people who understood the complexity of building new lives in a foreign place.

"This child will know where she comes from," declared Mrs. Singh, an elderly woman who had arrived from Guyana the same year as Sharifa. "She'll have American opportunities but Caribbean soul."

Two years later, Priya joined their family, arriving with less drama but just as much love. Where Saira was bold and demanding, Priya was thoughtful and observant, watching the world with serious dark eyes that seemed to see everything.

"Our little philosopher," Avinash called her, and indeed, even as a toddler, Priya would sit quietly and watch her older sister's antics with an expression of bemused tolerance.

The contrast between the sisters was apparent from the beginning. Saira attacked life head-on, crawling early, walking early, talking early, and always in motion. Priya was more deliberate, studying her world carefully before making moves. Where Saira would grab for toys with both hands, Priya would reach out tentatively, as if calculating the exact trajectory needed.

"They're like two sides of the same coin," Sharifa observed to Avinash one afternoon as they watched Saira trying to teach Priya to climb onto the couch.

"Good," he replied. "They'll balance each other out. Saira will teach Priya to be brave, and Priya will teach Saira to think before she leaps."

The house filled with the sounds of childhood—laughter and tears, the patter of small feet on hardwood floors, the constant chatter of little voices discovering language. Sharifa found herself busier than she'd ever been, yet more content. She had a routine now: early mornings with coffee and planning the day, afternoons in the small backyard watching the girls play, evenings when the whole family gathered around the dinner table.

Avinash proved to be an attentive father throughout those years. He would read to the girls before bed, his Guyanese accent giving the American storybooks a musical quality that made Saira giggle and Priya listen with rapt attention. On weekends, he would take them to Flushing Meadows Park, pushing them on swings and teaching them to catch butterflies with gentle hands.

"We're doing something right," Sharifa said one Sunday evening, watching Avinash help Saira with a puzzle while Priya colored at the kitchen table.

"We are," he agreed, looking up at her with the same warmth she remembered from their early days in Brooklyn. "This is what I dreamed of when I first wrote to you from America."

Sharifa had found work at a small accounting firm in Jamaica, Queens, recommended by one of the women from their Sunday dinner group. Her mathematical skills, which had served her so well as a teacher in Guyana, translated perfectly to bookkeeping and accounts receivable.

The interview had been intimidating—her first formal job interview in America—but Mr. Cohen, the office manager, had put her at ease immediately.

"You have teaching experience," he said, reviewing her carefully prepared resume. "That tells me you can explain things clearly and stay patient under pressure. Those are exactly the skills we need for collections."

"Collections?" Sharifa had asked, unfamiliar with the term.

"Calling customers who haven't paid their bills, convincing them to send payment. It requires diplomacy and persistence—teacher skills, exactly."

The work came naturally to her. There was something satisfying about organizing numbers, tracking payments, ensuring everything balanced to the penny. She discovered she had an aptitude for reading people's voices over the phone, for knowing exactly how much pressure to apply to get results without alienating customers.

"You have a gift," Mr. Cohen told her after her first month. "I've never seen anyone pick up our system so quickly. And your collection rate is already higher than our previous clerk's."

Sharifa enjoyed the work more than she'd expected. After years of caring for small children and managing a household, using her mind for professional challenges felt invigorating. She liked the puzzle aspect of accounting, the way numbers told stories about businesses and people's financial lives.

The office was small—just five employees—but the atmosphere was welcoming. Her colleagues were a mix of ages and backgrounds, united by their shared commitment to keeping their clients' financial records accurate and up-to-date.

"You speak so nicely to the difficult customers," observed Maria, the receptionist. "How do you stay so calm when they're yelling?"

"Practice," Sharifa replied diplomatically. She didn't mention that after dealing with toddler tantrums and sleepless nights, angry customers seemed relatively manageable.

The extra income made a significant difference in their lives. They were able to buy a second car, a used but reliable station wagon that made grocery shopping and family outings much easier. More importantly, they opened a savings account and watched it grow steadily each month.

"Look at this," Avinash said one evening, showing her their bank statement. "We've saved more in two years than my father saved in ten years of work in Georgetown."

Sharifa studied the numbers with satisfaction. She had always been careful with money, but now she was systematic about it. She kept detailed records of their expenses, planned their budget weeks in advance, and found ways to stretch every dollar without sacrificing quality of life.

"My mother always said Americans were wasteful with money," she told Avinash. "But I think the secret is having enough to plan with. When you're living week to week, you can't think about the future."

"Now we can think about the future," he agreed. "College for the girls, maybe a bigger house someday, visits back to Guyana."

The possibility of returning to Guyana, even for visits, filled Sharifa with complex emotions. She missed her family terribly, but she also felt proud of what she and Avinash had built in America. When she wrote letters home, she tried to balance honesty about their struggles with reassurance about their success.

"Tell Papa about Saira's English," she would write to her sister. "She speaks better than children twice her age. And Priya is already showing mathematical gifts—she can count to fifty and do simple addition."

The girls thrived in those years. Saira started kindergarten with the confidence of a child who had been loved and encouraged from birth. She made friends easily and came home with stories about her adventures that kept the dinner table lively with conversation.

"Today we learned about the pilgrims," Saira announced one October evening. "They came from far away, just like us!"

"That's right," Sharifa said, pleased that her daughter was beginning to understand their family's immigrant story. "They wanted a better life for their children, too."

Priya, though younger, was already showing signs of exceptional intelligence. She taught herself to read by watching Sharifa help Saira with her homework, and by age four could solve simple math problems that impressed even Avinash.

"She's going to be a doctor," Avinash predicted one evening after Priya had spent an hour carefully bandaging her doll's imaginary injuries.

"Or a scientist," Sharifa added, remembering how intently their younger daughter watched the way things worked—from the washing machine's cycles to the way flowers opened in their small garden.

"Or president," Mrs. Kowalski chimed in from over the fence. "Smart girls can be anything in America. That's why you came here, yes?"

"Yes," Sharifa agreed, feeling the truth of it in her bones. "That's exactly why we came here."

They developed traditions in those years that blended their Guyanese heritage with their new American identity. Sunday dinners became elaborate affairs, with Sharifa preparing dishes that combined her mother's recipes with ingredients available in Queens grocery stores. The girls would help in the kitchen, standing on step stools to reach the counter, their small hands learning to roll roti and mix curry powder.

"This is how your grandmother taught me," Sharifa would say, guiding Priya's hands as she kneaded dough. "And someday you'll teach your daughters."

"Will I go to Guyana?" Priya asked one afternoon, her serious eyes studying Sharifa's face.

"Someday," Sharifa promised. "When we've saved enough money for the whole family to travel together."

Holiday celebrations became particularly special as they created their own unique blend of traditions. They celebrated both Muslim and Hindu holidays, explaining to the girls that their family was blessed to have traditions from multiple cultures. Christmas became part of their routine too, as the girls insisted on joining their American classmates in decorating trees and exchanging gifts.

"We're creating our own culture," Avinash said one December evening, watching Saira hang ornaments while Priya carefully arranged the nativity scene they'd bought at Woolworth's.

"A mixed-up, wonderful culture," Sharifa agreed. "Caribbean and American, traditional and modern."

"Guyanese-American," Saira declared solemnly. "That's what I am."

"That's what we all are," Avinash said, lifting her up to place the star on top of their small tree.

The neighborhood embraced them gradually but genuinely. Mrs. Kowalski became particularly fond of the girls, teaching them to identify birds in the backyard and sharing vegetables from her impressive garden. The family across the street, the Johnsons, invited them to Fourth of July barbecues, where Sharifa's curried potato salad became a requested dish that disappeared before the hamburgers.

"Never had curry in potato salad before," Mr. Johnson admitted to Avinash one July afternoon. "But damn if it isn't the best thing I've ever tasted."

"Don't curse in front of the children," Mrs. Johnson scolded, but she was smiling. "Though I have to agree—Sharifa, you'll have to teach me how to make that."

Avinash joined a softball league at work and brought home stories of his teammates' good-natured ribbing about his cricket techniques. The cultural exchange went both ways, with Avinash teaching interested colleagues about Caribbean cricket while learning American baseball rules.

"They don't understand the beauty of a five-day test match," he told Sharifa after one particularly amusing practice session. "But they're good men. They've invited us to their Fourth of July party."

"Americans love their holidays," Sharifa observed. "Almost as much as we love ours."

Sharifa found a group of mothers at the girls' school who met for coffee on Wednesday mornings, sharing childrearing advice and local gossip with equal enthusiasm. The conversation was a mixture of practical parenting tips and gentle community gossip, always delivered with the understanding that they were all navigating the challenges of raising children in a rapidly changing world.

"Your girls are so well-behaved," commented Susan Martinez, whose own twin boys were notorious for their energy. "What's your secret?"

"Clear expectations and lots of love," Sharifa replied. "And making sure they know their father and I respect each other."

"I feel like we belong here," Sharifa told Avinash one evening as they sat on their small front porch, watching the girls chase fireflies in the twilight.

"We do belong here," he replied, taking her hand. "This is home now. Not Georgetown, not the place we left behind—this is where we're building our life."

The financial stability allowed them to think beyond mere survival for the first time since arriving in America. They talked about saving for the girls' college educations, about taking family vacations, about maybe buying a larger house someday when their savings account grew bigger.

"I want to take them to Niagara Falls," Avinash said one evening while reviewing their budget. "Show them one of America's natural wonders."

"And the Statue of Liberty," Sharifa added. "They should see the lady who welcomed us to this country."

Sharifa even began to dream about visiting Guyana again, showing her daughters where their parents had grown up, introducing them to grandparents and aunts and uncles who existed only in stories and letters.

"When they're older," she told Avinash. "When they can appreciate what we left behind to give them this life."

These were the years when laughter came easily, when problems seemed manageable, when the future stretched ahead bright with possibility. Sharifa would wake each morning with a sense of gratitude that still surprised her—gratitude for her healthy children, her loving husband, her comfortable home, her meaningful work.

"Ten years," she said to herself one morning in 1978, standing in her kitchen making breakfast for her family. Ten years since she'd arrived in America frightened and uncertain. Ten years since she'd married a man she barely knew for practical reasons. Ten years of building something beautiful from nothing more than hope and determination.

She didn't know then that the good years were about to end, that the man humming contentedly in their bedroom as he dressed for work would soon become a stranger who frightened her.

But on that morning, with Avinash calling out cheerful good-mornings to the girls and Saira trying to braid Priya's hair while Priya practiced her multiplication tables, Sharifa felt nothing but gratitude for the life they had built together in Queens.

The house was filled with the sounds of a happy family beginning another day, and for ten perfect years, that had been enough.

Chapter 8
The Fracture

The changes started so gradually that Sharifa almost missed them. A missed dinner here, a late night there, the scent of unfamiliar perfume clinging to Avinash's shirts when she gathered laundry. She told herself it was work stress, or the natural evolution of a fifteen-year marriage. She told herself many things in those early months of 1979, because the alternative was too frightening to acknowledge.

"You're working late again," she said one Thursday evening when Avinash called to say he wouldn't be home for dinner.

"Big project," he replied, his voice distant in a way that had become familiar. "You know how it is."

But Sharifa didn't know how it was. His previous late nights had been accompanied by frustrated complaints about deadlines or difficult clients. He would come home exhausted but talkative, sharing the details of his workday over reheated dinner. Now there was just silence, followed by excuses that felt rehearsed and hollow.

"What kind of project?" she asked, trying to keep her voice neutral.

"Technical stuff. You wouldn't understand."

The dismissal stung more than she expected. Avinash had never spoken to her with such casual condescension before. For fifteen years, he had respected her intelligence, had asked for her opinion on work matters, had treated her as an equal partner in their marriage.

"Try me," she said.

"Sharifa, I'm tired. Can we not do this tonight?"

The phone clicked dead before she could respond, leaving her standing in the kitchen with dinner growing cold and questions multiplying in her mind.

The girls, now seven and five, sensed the shift even if they couldn't name it. Saira became more clingy, insisting on sleeping in Sharifa's bed when Avinash wasn't home. Priya grew quieter, her serious eyes tracking the tension that had begun to fill their house like smoke from a fire no one could locate.

"Where's Papa?" Saira asked one Saturday morning when Avinash had left early, claiming he needed to catch up on paperwork at the office.

"Working," Sharifa said, but the word felt hollow in her mouth. She had driven past his office building the previous weekend while running errands and seen the empty parking lot, the dark windows of the engineering firm where he supposedly spent so many hours.

"On Saturday?" Priya looked up from her coloring book with the penetrating gaze that never missed anything.

"Sometimes adults have to work on weekends," Sharifa said, hating herself for the lie.

"Mrs. Johnson says Mr. Johnson never works on Saturdays," Saira observed. "She says Saturday is family day."

"Every family is different," Sharifa replied, but she found herself wondering what had happened to their family days, when Saturday mornings had meant pancakes and park visits and lazy afternoons in their small backyard.

The first real confirmation came in March, when Sharifa answered the phone to a woman's voice asking for "Avi."

"I'm sorry, you have the wrong number," Sharifa said automatically.

"Is this 718-555-4729?" the voice persisted. It was a young voice, confident and slightly breathless with laughter. "Avi Sharma?"

Sharifa felt her world tilt. No one called her husband Avi. His family in Guyana called him Avinash, his coworkers called him Vince, she called him by his full name or sometimes "darling" in private moments. But Avi was intimate, playful—the kind of nick-name a woman would use when she was comfortable with a man, when she knew him well enough to shorten his name into some-thing affectionate.

"He's not available," Sharifa managed, her voice sounding strange to her own ears.

"Oh." The woman sounded disappointed but not surprised. "Well, tell him Denise called. He has my number."

The casual assumption that Sharifa would pass along the message was perhaps the most insulting part. This Denise clearly expected to be accommodated, as if her claims on Avinash's attention were legiti-mate and recognized.

"I'll tell him," Sharifa said, and hung up.

When she confronted Avinash that evening, he dismissed it easily. "A colleague from work. You misunderstood the situation."

"She called you Avi."

"It's a nickname some people use. Don't make something out of nothing, Sharifa."

But Sharifa hadn't misunderstood. She had understood perfectly, perhaps for the first time in months. The late nights, the changed behavior, the casual dismissal of her concerns—it all fit together into a picture she had been refusing to see.

"How long?" she asked quietly.

"How long what?" But his eyes wouldn't meet hers, and that told her everything she needed to know.

The drinking started around the same time, or perhaps she sim-ply began noticing it. Avinash had always enjoyed a beer with dinner, especially on Friday nights when the workweek was finished. But now he came home with whiskey on his breath and unsteady steps. He would pour himself a drink before greeting the girls, another with dinner, and often a third while watching television.

"You're drinking too much," Sharifa said one evening after he'd nearly fallen asleep in his chair during the evening news.

"I'm relaxing," he replied, his words slightly slurred. "A man deserves to relax in his own home after working hard all day."

"The girls notice," she said softly.

"The girls need to mind their own business," he snapped, louder than necessary. "And so do you."

Saira appeared in the doorway at that moment, her pajamas wrinkled from sleep, her face concerned. "Is everything okay?"

"Everything's fine, beta," Sharifa said quickly, moving to guide her daughter back toward the bedroom. "Papa's just tired from work."

But over Saira's head, she caught Avinash's cold stare, as if she had somehow betrayed him by comforting their daughter.

The fights began in whispers, conducted in the kitchen after the girls had gone to bed. Sharifa would ask where he'd been, and Avinash would respond with accusations of her own. She was too suspicious, too controlling, too concerned with things that weren't her business.

"I work hard for this family," he would say, his voice rising despite her gestures for quiet. "I provide for you, for them. What more do you want?"

"I want my husband back," Sharifa wanted to say, but the words stuck in her throat. The man standing in her kitchen, smelling of alcohol and another woman's perfume, wasn't the father who had once read bedtime stories with infinite patience, who had taught Saira to ride a bicycle and helped Priya build elaborate block towers.

"I want honesty," she said instead.

"You want to control every aspect of my life," he replied. "You want to know where I am every minute, who I talk to, what I do with my time. That's not a marriage, Sharifa. That's a prison."

The accusation hung between them like a physical barrier. Was she being controlling? Was it unreasonable to expect her husband to come home for dinner with his family? To want to know why he was working late so many nights? To question why strange women were calling their house asking for him by pet names?

"I just want us to be a family again," she said.

"We are a family. But that doesn't mean I have to account for every moment of my day to you."

The religious differences, which had been managed peacefully for years, suddenly became weapons in their escalating war. Avinash began making comments about Sharifa's faith, about her "stubborn refusal" to embrace his family's traditions completely.

"The girls are confused," he said one Sunday morning when Sharifa prepared to take them to the mosque for Eid prayers. "All this mixing of religions. They don't know what they believe."

"They believe in love," Sharifa replied, adjusting Priya's best dress. "They believe their parents respect each other's faiths."

"Do we?" Avinash asked, and something in his tone made Sharifa look at him sharply.

The question hung between them, loaded with implications that frightened her. For fifteen years, their religious differences had been a source of interesting discussions and rich cultural experiences for their children. Now, suddenly, her Muslim faith was being treated as an obstacle to family harmony.

"I've never asked you to change your beliefs," Sharifa said carefully.

"Haven't you? Every time you take them to the mosque, you're telling them that my faith isn't enough. Every time you pray in Arabic instead of Sanskrit, you're showing them that you don't respect their father's traditions."

"That's not true, and you know it."

"Is it? When was the last time you attended a Hindu ceremony with me? When was the last time you showed any interest in the religion your daughters are supposed to inherit?"

The argument continued in the car, conducted in tense whispers while the girls sat in the backseat, until finally Avinash pulled over to the curb three blocks from the mosque.

"Get out," he said.

"What?"

"You want to go to your mosque so badly? Walk. The girls and I will go home."

"Avinash, don't be ridiculous. It's seven blocks."

"Should have thought of that before you decided to be so stubborn about this."

Sharifa looked back at her daughters, who were watching the argument with wide, frightened eyes. The idea of creating a bigger scene in front of them was worse than the humiliation of walking to the mosque alone.

"Fine," she said, gathering her purse and opening the car door.

She heard Saira's voice calling "Mama!" as Avinash drove away, but she didn't look back. The seven-block walk to the mosque gave her plenty of time to wonder when her husband had become someone who would abandon his wife on a street corner to make a point about religious authority.

Avinash began to demand changes that felt calculated to erase her identity. The girls should focus more on Hindu traditions, he said. They should learn Sanskrit prayers instead of Arabic ones. They should understand that his faith was the faith of their father, and therefore took precedence in their household.

"We agreed," Sharifa reminded him during one particularly heated argument. "Before we married, we agreed they would learn about both cultures."

"That was before I realized how stubborn you would be about maintaining your separateness from this family."

"My faith isn't separate from this family. It's part of what makes this family what it is."

"No," Avinash said coldly. "What makes this family is my work, my income, my decisions. Your job is to support those things, not to fight them."

The word 'stubborn' became his favorite weapon, deployed whenever Sharifa expressed any opinion that differed from his own. Sharifa was stubborn about religion, stubborn about wanting to know where he spent his evenings, stubborn about expecting him to come home for dinner. Everything she had once been praised for—her independence, her strength, her convictions—was now cast as a character flaw that threatened their marriage.

"You want to control everything," he would say during their late-night arguments. "The money, the children, my time. You're like a prison warden."

"I want to be your partner," Sharifa would reply. "I want us to make decisions together."

64

"I make the decisions. You support them. That's how marriage works."

Sharifa began to recognize the signs of his moods with the precision of a meteorologist tracking storm systems. On good days, he would come home relatively sober and make an effort with the girls, helping with homework or playing board games. He would kiss Sharifa hello and ask about her day at work, and for brief moments she could pretend they were still the couple who had fallen in love in Brooklyn.

On bad days, he would arrive drunk and angry, looking for reasons to start fights. His eyes would scan the house for imperfections—toys not properly put away, dishes still in the sink, homework assignments spread across the kitchen table. Every small sign of normal family life became evidence of Sharifa's failure to maintain proper order.

She learned to read his face when he walked through the door, to gauge whether the evening would be peaceful or explosive. She began sending the girls to their rooms early on the bad nights, making excuses about homework or early bedtimes while she tried to manage whatever crisis was brewing in her husband's mind.

"Why is Papa angry so much?" Priya asked one evening after a particularly loud argument had ended with Avinash storming out of the house.

"He's just tired from work," Sharifa said, the lie bitter on her tongue.

"Adults shouldn't yell," Priya said matter-of-factly. "My teacher says using your words nicely is better than yelling."

"Your teacher is very smart," Sharifa agreed, wishing Avinash could hear his five-year-old daughter's wisdom.

"If Papa is tired, maybe he should sleep more instead of staying out late," Saira suggested with the innocent logic of childhood.

The observation was so accurate that Sharifa had to turn away to hide her expression. Even her seven-year-old could see what was happening to their family, could identify the source of the tension that had infected their once-happy home.

The financial control began subtly, introduced through conversations about "responsible spending" and "family priorities." Avinash,

65

who had once praised Sharifa's careful money management, began questioning every purchase, no matter how small or necessary.

"Why did the girls need new shoes?" he asked one evening, holding up the receipt from their shopping trip. "What was wrong with their old ones?"

"They've grown out of them," Sharifa replied patiently. "Children's feet grow quickly."

"Seems like they just got new shoes."

"That was six months ago."

"Six months? You're spending money on shoes every six months? Do you have any idea how much money that is over a year?"

The mathematical precision of his criticism might have been amusing if it weren't so obviously designed to make her feel guilty for meeting their children's basic needs. Sharifa, who managed the household budget with careful attention to every dollar, knew exactly how much they spent on children's shoes, children's clothes, children's everything. It was all within the budget they had agreed upon, all necessary expenses for a growing family.

"I can show you the budget," she offered.

"The budget you created," he said dismissively. "Maybe it's time I took a more active role in managing our money."

The phrase "our money" was particularly galling, since Sharifa's salary contributed nearly forty percent of their household income. But pointing that out would only escalate the argument, so she remained silent.

"I make most of the money," he continued, as if reading her thoughts. "I should have the final say in how it's spent."

Sharifa's job, which had once been a source of pride and independence, became another point of contention. Avinash complained that she worked too much, that the girls needed their mother home. But when she suggested reducing her hours, he worried about the lost income and its impact on their financial goals.

"You can't have it both ways," Sharifa finally said during one particularly circular argument.

"I can have it any way I want," Avinash replied. "This is my house."

The possessive pronouns multiplied with each passing week. His house, his money, his children, his decisions. Sharifa found herself being erased from the family narrative, becoming a supporting character in her own life.

She began to understand that the man who had courted her so patiently, who had written those gentle letters from America, who had fallen in love with her slowly and sweetly in their Brooklyn apartment—that man had been real, but he was disappearing. In his place was someone she didn't recognize, someone who seemed to resent her very existence.

The worst part was the unpredictability. Just when Sharifa had accepted that her marriage was ending, Avinash would have a good day. He would bring flowers home for no reason, play with the girls until they collapsed in giggles, make love to her with something approaching his old tenderness.

"See?" he would say afterward, holding her close in their darkened bedroom. "You worry too much. We're fine."

But they weren't fine, and Sharifa was beginning to realize that the good days weren't signs of improvement—they were just breaks in the storm. The man who brought her flowers on Tuesday was the same man who would berate her for overcooking dinner on Wednesday, who would question her loyalty on Thursday, who would come home drunk and defensive on Friday.

The community that had once embraced their family began to notice the changes, though no one spoke about them directly. Mrs. Kowalski stopped offering unsolicited advice over the fence. The other mothers at school seemed to maintain more distance during their casual conversations.

"Everything alright at home?" Maria from work asked one Monday morning when Sharifa arrived looking particularly exhausted.

"Fine," Sharifa replied automatically. "Just tired."

But it wasn't fine, and she wasn't just tired. She was emotionally exhausted from walking on eggshells, from trying to anticipate and prevent her husband's moods, from maintaining the fiction that their marriage was solid while it crumbled around her.

By the end of 1979, the pattern was established. Avinash would disappear for hours without explanation, return home drunk and defensive, start fights over trivial matters, then occasionally surprise everyone with moments of his former self. The girls learned to walk carefully around him, to speak quietly when he was home, to save their exuberant stories for when he was gone.

Sharifa found herself making excuses to friends and neighbors, covering for his absences and explaining away his mood swings. She became expert at deflecting questions about his work schedule, at laughing off concerns about her own increasingly hollow appearance.

"Marriage is hard work," she would say when Mrs. Kowalski asked if everything was alright. "Some seasons are more difficult than others."

But seasons were supposed to change, and Sharifa was beginning to fear that winter had come to stay.

The fifteen-year mark of their marriage passed without acknowledgment. Once, Avinash had marked every anniversary with dinner at their favorite restaurant, with small gifts and thoughtful gestures. He would reminisce about their wedding day, about the nervous young woman who had married him more for opportunity than love, about how grateful he was that she had learned to love him anyway.

Now, December 15th came and went like any other day, notable only for the fight they had about Saira's report card and the fact that Avinash didn't come home until three in the morning. When he finally stumbled into their bedroom, reeking of alcohol and cigarettes, Sharifa pretended to be asleep rather than confront him about where he had been.

Lying in bed that night, listening to his unsteady breathing beside her, Sharifa made a mental note of the date. Later, she would mark it as the end of the good years and the beginning of something much darker.

But she didn't know yet how dark it would become.

Chapter 9
Secret Endurance

The bruises were always in places no one would see. Avinash had learned to be strategic in his violence, careful to preserve the facade of respectability that kept their neighbors smiling and their friends unsuspecting. A grip too tight around her arm, leaving finger-shaped marks that her long sleeves would cover. A shove that sent her stumbling into the kitchen counter, the edge catching her ribs in a way that would leave her wincing for days. A backhand that left her lip split but not obviously swollen—just enough to remind her of his power without advertising it to the world.

"You're clumsy lately," Mrs. Kowalski observed one morning when Sharifa winced while hanging laundry. "Maybe you need to get your eyes checked."

"Maybe I do," Sharifa agreed, knowing the real problem wasn't her vision but her husband's fists.

By 1981, the violence had become as routine as their morning coffee or evening news. It followed a predictable pattern that Sharifa had learned to read like a familiar script: Avinash would come home drunk, find something to criticize, escalate to shouting, and then cross the line into physical punishment for whatever transgression he'd invented.

The girls, now nine and seven, learned to disappear when Papa came home in his dark moods. They developed an early warning system without ever discussing it explicitly—watching for Sharifa's subtle signals that meant retreat to their bedrooms and close the door. Sometimes Sharifa envied their ability to escape; she had nowhere to hide.

"I'm sorry, Mama," Saira whispered one morning, finding Sharifa gingerly touching a bruise on her ribcage while getting dressed for work. "I should have cleaned my room better yesterday."

"Oh, beta," Sharifa pulled her older daughter close, her heart breaking at the guilt in the child's voice. "Papa's anger isn't because of you. It's never because of you or your sister."

"But he said—"

"What Papa says when he's angry doesn't reflect what he really thinks," Sharifa interrupted, hating herself for the lie even as she spoke it. "He's just... frustrated with grown-up things. Work things. Things that have nothing to do with you girls."

But the truth was more complicated. Everything was because of something, in Avinash's world. Dinner served five minutes late, a toy left in the hallway, a bill that came in higher than expected—any small imperfection became evidence of Sharifa's fundamental failure as a wife and mother.

"You can't do anything right," he would say, punctuating his words with slaps or shoves. "I work all day, and I come home to chaos."

The chaos he described was invisible to everyone else. Their house remained neat and organized, the girls were well-behaved and consistently clean, dinner was prepared and waiting each evening. But perfection, Sharifa learned, was a moving target when the person judging you wanted to find fault.

"Look at this," Avinash said one evening, pointing to a water spot on a drinking glass that Priya had washed and put away. "This is what I'm talking about. No attention to detail. No pride in your work."

"She's seven years old," Sharifa replied quietly. "She's doing her best to help."

"Don't make excuses for poor work. If she's old enough to wash dishes, she's old enough to wash them properly."

70

He made Priya rewash every glass in the cabinet while he supervised, pointing out imaginary spots and water marks until the child was in tears. Sharifa watched from the doorway, torn between protecting her daughter and knowing that intervening would only make things worse for everyone.

The isolation began gradually, introduced through Avinash's growing commentary on her friendships and social interactions. He started questioning why she needed to have coffee with the women from the girls' school, why she spent so much time chatting with Mrs. Kowalski over the fence.

"You talk too much," he would say after she returned from any social interaction. "You tell them our business."

"I don't discuss our private matters," Sharifa would protest.

"Don't lie to me," he would snap. "I see how you are with them. Always complaining, always making me look bad."

Eventually, it became easier to avoid the conversations altogether. Sharifa began declining invitations to coffee meetings, making excuses for why she couldn't join the other mothers for their Wednesday morning gatherings. She kept her interactions with neighbors brief and superficial, afraid that her face might give away secrets she wasn't ready to share.

"We haven't seen you at coffee in weeks," commented Janet Morrison, another mother from Saira's class. "Everything okay at home?"

"Just busy," Sharifa replied, forcing a smile. "Work has been demanding, and the girls have so many activities."

"Well, you know where to find us if you need to talk," Janet said gently. "Sometimes it helps to have other women to bounce things off of."

The kindness in her voice almost broke Sharifa's resolve to keep her problems private. For a moment, she imagined telling Janet everything—about the drinking, the violence, the way her once-loving husband had transformed into someone she no longer recognized. But what would be the point? Janet had her own family, her own problems. Sharifa's marriage was her responsibility to fix or endure.

The train rides to work became her sanctuary and her torture.

71

Sitting in the subway car during her morning commute, Sharifa would allow herself to cry quietly, her tears hidden behind a newspaper or obscured by the crowded car. The rhythm of the rails provided a soundtrack to her grief, and the strangers around her offered the paradoxical comfort of anonymity.

In the mornings, she would cry about the night before—whatever fresh humiliation or violence had been inflicted, whatever new way Avinash had found to diminish her sense of self-worth. In the evenings, she would cry about going home, about facing whatever mood would greet her when she walked through the door.

Sometimes, when the bruises were particularly bad or her emotional state was especially fragile, she would catch other passengers looking at her with concern or curiosity. She learned to sit in ways that minimized the visibility of finger-shaped marks on her arms, to position herself so that handprint bruises on her neck weren't obvious to casual observers.

"You okay, honey?" an elderly woman asked one morning when Sharifa's quiet crying had become audible.

"Just tired," Sharifa replied, forcing a smile that felt like a physical effort. "Long night with sick children."

The lies came so easily now that they frightened her. She had become fluent in deception, crafting explanations for every mark, every wince, every moment of visible pain. She told her supervisor at work that she'd fallen down the stairs when her wrist was sprained from Avinash twisting it. She explained a black eye as the result of walking into a cabinet door in the dark. She blamed a limp on slipping in the bathtub.

"You should be more careful," Mr. Cohen said with genuine concern after the cabinet door explanation. "Maybe you need better lighting at home."

"Yes," Sharifa agreed. "Better lighting would help a lot."

If only it were that simple, she thought. If only the darkness in her house could be fixed with brighter bulbs instead of requiring the complete transformation of the man she had once loved.

At work, she threw herself into the numbers with desperate

intensity. Accounts receivable became a refuge where everything made sense, where problems had clear solutions, where her competence was unquestioned and appreciated. She was promoted to credit manager, a position that required calling customers about overdue payments—a task that felt almost laughably simple compared to navigating Avinash's moods.

"You're the best we've ever had at collections," Mr. Cohen told her during her performance review. "I don't know how you do it. You get people to pay who've been ignoring our calls for months."

Sharifa knew exactly how she did it. After years of carefully managing Avinash's temper, convincing angry customers to pay their bills was nothing. She had learned to read voices, to detect the subtle shifts in tone that preceded either cooperation or explosion. She had become an expert in de-escalation, in finding the exact words that would calm a volatile situation.

"Mrs. Patterson," she would say to a particularly difficult customer, "I understand you're frustrated about this bill. Let's see if we can work together to find a solution that makes sense for your situation."

The skills that made her valuable at work made her a target at home. Avinash resented her success, her steady income, her growing confidence in professional settings. He began to undermine her achievements, dismissing her promotions as "charity" and her salary as "pocket change."

"You think you're so important," he would sneer when she came home with news of a successful day. "But you're nothing without me. Don't forget that."

"I never said I was more important," Sharifa would reply carefully.

"You don't have to say it. It's written all over your face. You walk around here like you're better than this family, like your little job makes you independent."

The accusations were designed to confuse her, to make her question her own perceptions and motivations. Was she becoming arrogant? Was her job success making her a worse wife and mother? The self-doubt was perhaps more damaging than the physical violence, because it made her complicit in her own diminishment.

The reminders of her dependence became constant. He controlled the bank accounts, despite her income contributing nearly half of their household expenses. He made decisions about major purchases without consulting her. He threatened regularly to "throw her out" if she didn't show proper appreciation for all he provided.

"Where would you go?" he would ask during their fights, his voice heavy with mock concern. "Who would want you? A woman with two children and no family in this country?"

The questions haunted her because she didn't have good answers. Her family in Guyana was an ocean away and largely disappointed in her life choices. Her friends in Queens were casual acquaintances, not the kind of people you could turn to in crisis. Her daughters needed stability, education, a future—things she couldn't provide alone on her salary.

"You need me," Avinash would continue when she didn't respond to his rhetorical questions. "The girls need me. This house, this life, everything you have—it exists because I allow it to exist."

The physical abuse escalated slowly, as if Avinash were testing her limits and his own capacity for violence. A slap became a punch. A push became a shove down the stairs. Grabbing became choking, just for a few seconds, just long enough to make his point about who held the power in their relationship.

"You made me do this," he would say afterward, his voice heavy with manufactured regret. "If you weren't so stubborn, so argumentative, I wouldn't have to discipline you."

The word 'discipline' made Sharifa's skin crawl. She wasn't a child to be corrected; she was a grown woman being terrorized in her own home. But saying so only provoked worse violence, so she learned to absorb his twisted logic in silence.

"I don't want to hurt you," he would continue during these post-violence speeches. "But someone has to teach you how to be a proper wife. Someone has to help you understand your place in this family."

The girls began showing signs of the strain, developing behaviors that broke Sharifa's heart even as she felt powerless to address their root cause. Saira, always outgoing and confident, became withdrawn at school. Her teacher called to express concern about her declining participation in class activities and her reluctance to speak up during group discussions.

"She seems anxious," Mrs. Patterson explained during a parent conference that Sharifa attended alone. "Like she's worried about something at home."

"We've been having some... adjustments," Sharifa said carefully. "Her father has been working longer hours, and I think she misses him."

"Children are very sensitive to family stress," Mrs. Patterson said gently. "Even when parents think they're hiding it well."

The observation was both comforting and terrifying. Comforting because it meant Sharifa wasn't imagining the impact on her daughters. Terrifying because it meant she was failing to protect them from the chaos of their home life.

Priya, meanwhile, threw herself into her studies with an intensity that worried Sharifa. Even at seven, she seemed to understand that academic achievement might be her ticket out of a situation she couldn't yet name.

"I'm going to be a doctor," Priya announced one evening over dinner, her young voice filled with fierce determination. "Doctors help people who are hurt."

Avinash laughed, but there was no warmth in the sound. "Doctors need families who can afford medical school. We'll see how smart you really are when it counts."

The casual cruelty of dismissing their daughter's dreams was another kind of violence, Sharifa realized. He was teaching the girls that their aspirations meant nothing, that their worth was determined by his approval alone.

Some nights, after particularly brutal episodes, Sharifa would lie awake planning escapes. She would calculate how much money she had in her personal checking account, think about apartments she might be able to afford, imagine conversations with sympathetic landlords who would overlook her lack of credit history. But morning always brought reality: she couldn't support two children on her salary alone, couldn't provide them with the stability they needed while rebuilding her entire life from scratch.

The mathematics of escape were as brutal as the violence itself. Rent, utilities, food, clothing, childcare, medical expenses—the numbers never worked out in her favor. Even with her steady job, she would be barely surviving, and the girls would suffer the consequences of her decision to leave.

"I could go back to school," she would think during her darkest moments. "Learn new skills, get a better job." But when? How? Who would watch the girls while she attended classes? How would she pay for education while supporting a household?

The isolation had another consequence she hadn't anticipated. Without friends to confide in, without family to call for support, Sharifa began to doubt her own perceptions. When Avinash told her she was overreacting, being too sensitive, making mountains out of molehills, part of her began to believe him.

"You're crazy," he would say when she flinched at his raised hand. "I wasn't going to hit you. You're paranoid."

But the bruises on her body told a different story, even when her mind began to question the evidence. She started taking photographs of the worst injuries, hiding the Polaroid pictures in a shoebox under her side of the bed. The visual proof helped anchor her to reality when Avinash's gaslighting threatened to make her doubt her own experiences.

The worst part wasn't the physical pain, which was considerable, or even the emotional devastation of watching her marriage disintegrate. The worst part was the way the violence changed her relationship with her daughters. She found herself snapping at them when they were too loud, too demanding, too childlike. She was always listening for Avinash's key in the door, always calculating whether their behavior would provoke his anger.

"Mama's tired," became her constant refrain. "Play quietly. Don't make noise. Daddy's had a long day."

She was teaching them to tiptoe through their own lives, and she hated herself for it almost as much as she hated him for creating the situation. They were learning that their natural exuberance was something to be contained, that their father's moods took precedence over their own needs for expression and play.

"Why can't we sing?" Priya asked one afternoon when Sharifa had shushed them for the third time.

"Papa is sleeping," Sharifa replied, though it was only four in the afternoon and Avinash was supposedly at work.

"But we like to sing," Saira protested. "It makes us happy."

"I know, beta. But we have to think about others too."

The conversation broke her heart because she could see them processing the message: their happiness was less important than avoiding their father's displeasure. She was raising them to be fearful, to prioritize other people's comfort over their own authentic selves.

By 1982, crying had become as routine as breathing. She cried on the train to work, thinking about the night before. She cried at her desk when she thought no one was looking, overwhelmed by the effort of maintaining her professional facade. She cried on the train home, dreading whatever mood would greet her when she walked through the door. She cried herself to sleep, muffling the sound with her pillow so the girls wouldn't hear.

The tears were her secret companion, her only honest response to a life that had become unrecognizable. They reminded her that somewhere inside the carefully controlled exterior she'd learned to present to the world, the real Sharifa still existed—bruised and frightened, but not yet broken.

The breaking point was coming, though she didn't know it yet. The spiral of violence was accelerating, and Avinash's control was becoming more absolute with each passing month. Soon, the strategic bruises wouldn't be enough to satisfy his need to dominate. Soon, the careful facade would crack, and the world would see what her marriage had really become.

But for now, she endured. She went to work each day and excelled at her job. She came home each evening and tried to protect her daughters from the worst of their father's rage. She cried her secret tears and planned impossible escapes and convinced herself that somehow, some way, things would get better.

They wouldn't get better.

They would get much, much worse.

Chapter 10
The Stairs

The morning of March 15, 1983, began like so many others—with Sharifa moving quietly through the house, trying not to wake Avinash before she had coffee made and breakfast prepared. He had come home past midnight, drunk and belligerent, and the careful silence of morning felt like a temporary truce in a war that never truly ended.

She had heard him stumbling through the front door around 12:30, followed by the sound of him knocking over the umbrella stand in the hallway. His muttered curses had been loud enough to wake her, but she had remained perfectly still in their bed, feigning sleep to avoid whatever confrontation he might be seeking.

Saira, now eleven, helped pack lunches while Priya, nine, organized her school books with the methodical precision that had become her coping mechanism. Both girls had learned to read the atmospheric pressure of their home, to gauge whether Papa would emerge from the bedroom like a storm or merely a gray cloud.

"He's still sleeping," Saira whispered, glancing toward the closed bedroom door.

"Good," Sharifa replied, though she knew the peace was temporary. Avinash would wake hungover and angry, looking for someone to blame for the pounding in his head and the sour taste in his mouth.

"Maybe he'll sleep until we get home from school," Priya said hopefully.

"Maybe," Sharifa agreed, though she doubted it. Avinash had to work today, which meant he would force himself up regardless of how he felt. And the worse he felt, the more likely he was to take it out on whoever was available.

The girls caught their school bus just as Avinash's alarm began buzzing insistently in the bedroom. Sharifa braced herself, listening to his movements—the heavy footsteps, the muttered curses, the sound of drawers being yanked open and slammed shut. Each noise was a weather report on his mood, and today's forecast looked stormy.

When he emerged thirty minutes later, his face was thunderous. His hair stuck up at odd angles, his eyes were bloodshot and rimmed with the telltale puffiness of too much alcohol, and he moved with the careful deliberation of someone fighting nausea.

"Coffee," he said, not bothering with pleasantries or even looking at her directly.

Sharifa had already poured it, had already set it on the table with his preferred breakfast—two eggs over easy, toast with butter, orange juice. But Avinash seemed determined to find fault, his eyes scanning the table for something to criticize.

"It's cold," he said after one sip, though steam was still rising from the cup.

"I can make fresh—"

"Don't." His voice was sharp enough to cut. "I don't have time for your incompetence this morning."

Sharifa bit back her response. She had learned that defending herself only provided more ammunition for his attacks. Better to let him eat in silence and leave for work without a fight, to hope that eight hours away would improve his mood.

But Avinash wasn't finished. He pushed the coffee cup away with enough force to slosh the liquid onto the table, then fixed her with the cold stare that had become so familiar.

"You know what your problem is?" he said, though the question

80

was clearly rhetorical. "You think you're better than this family. You think your little job makes you important."

Sharifa continued wiping down the counter, hoping her silence would discourage whatever tirade was building. She had learned to make herself small during these moments, to become as invisible as possible until the storm passed.

"I'm talking to you," Avinash said, his voice rising. "The least you could do is look at me when I'm speaking."

Reluctantly, Sharifa turned to face him. His eyes held the particular combination of rage and self-pity that she had come to dread. This wasn't going to be a quick morning outburst; this was going to be something worse.

"Fifteen years," he continued, standing up from the table with deliberate slowness. "Fifteen years I've provided for you, given you a home, given you status in this country. And what do I get in return? A wife who thinks she's too good to show proper respect."

The accusations were familiar, a greatest hits collection of all her supposed failures. Sharifa had heard variations of this speech dozens of times, but something in Avinash's posture suggested today would be different. He was positioning himself between her and the kitchen doorway, blocking her escape route.

"You walk around this house like you own it," he continued, taking a step closer. "Acting like you're doing me a favor by living here. Well, let me remind you of something—this is my house. Everything in it belongs to me. Including you."

The possessive language had escalated over the years, but the word 'including' sent ice through Sharifa's veins. She wasn't his possession, wasn't property to be owned and controlled. The thought must have shown on her face because Avinash's expression darkened further.

"You disagree?" he asked, his voice deceptively quiet. "You think you have some kind of independence? Some kind of choice in how you behave in my home?"

"I think I deserve basic respect," Sharifa said, the words escaping before she could stop them.

The silence that followed was dense with danger. Avinash's jaw tightened, his hands curling into fists at his sides. Sharifa realized she had made a crucial mistake—she had challenged him directly, had refused to accept his version of reality.

"Respect?" he repeated, his voice beginning to rise again. "You want to talk about respect? How about the respect you owe your husband? How about the gratitude you should show for everything I've given you?"

He was moving closer now, backing her toward the stove. Sharifa's heart began to race as she recognized the familiar escalation pattern. But something felt different this time, more dangerous than their usual fights.

"How about the respect you should show by not questioning my authority in my own house?" His voice was getting louder with each word, but Sharifa could hear him trying to control the volume, aware that neighbors might hear.

"I wasn't questioning—" she began, but the attempt at de-escalation came too late.

"Don't lie to me!" The words exploded out of him, loud enough that Mrs. Kowalski next door surely heard. "You questioned me! You think you deserve respect? You think you've earned the right to have opinions about how I run this family?"

The first blow came without warning, a backhanded slap that snapped her head to the side and brought tears to her eyes. But instead of the usual pause that followed his violence—the moment where he would gauge whether his point had been made—Avinash seemed to gain momentum.

"You ungrateful—" Another slap, harder this time, the sound echoing in the small kitchen. "You think your little job makes you independent? You think you could survive without me?"

Sharifa tried to move away, to create distance between them, but the kitchen was small and Avinash was blocking her path. When she attempted to step around him, he grabbed her arm with bruising force.

"Where do you think you're going?" His grip tightened, fingers digging into the bruises from last week's fight. "We're not finished talking."

"The girls will be home soon," Sharifa said, though it was a lie. School had just started; they wouldn't return for hours.

"The girls," Avinash repeated mockingly. "Always hiding behind the girls. Using them as an excuse to avoid dealing with your responsibilities as a wife."

He shoved her backward, harder than usual, and Sharifa stumbled against the kitchen counter. The edge caught her hip, sending sharp pain through her side. But Avinash wasn't satisfied with her obvious discomfort.

"You want to know what I think?" he said, advancing on her again. "I think you've forgotten who's in charge here. I think you need a reminder."

The next series of blows came in rapid succession—slaps, punches, pushes that sent her careening into appliances and walls. Sharifa tried to protect herself, raising her arms to shield her face, but Avinash seemed determined to overwhelm her defenses.

"Stop," she gasped between hits. "Please, Avinash, stop."

But her pleas only seemed to enrage him further. He grabbed her by the shoulders and shook her so violently that her teeth chattered.

"Don't tell me to stop!" he shouted, his control completely gone now. "You don't get to give me orders! You don't get to tell me what to do in my own house!"

Sharifa saw the punch coming but couldn't move fast enough to avoid it completely. His fist caught her in the ribs, driving the air from her lungs and sending electric pain through her torso. She doubled over, gasping, trying to catch her breath.

"Get up," Avinash commanded. "Get up and look at me when I'm talking to you."

But Sharifa couldn't straighten, couldn't breathe properly. The pain in her ribs was sharp and constant, suggesting something might be broken or at least severely bruised. She remained hunched over, one hand pressed to her side.

"I said get up!" Avinash grabbed her hair, yanking her head back with enough force to make her cry out. "You want to act like a victim? I'll give you something to feel victimized about."

He dragged her toward the kitchen doorway, his grip on her hair making it impossible to resist without ripping the strands from her scalp. Sharifa's scalp burned, her ribs ached, and terror was beginning to override her ability to think clearly.

They reached the bottom of the stairs, and for a moment Sharifa thought he was going to force her upstairs, continue the assault in the privacy of their bedroom. But instead, Avinash positioned himself behind her, one hand still tangled in her hair, the other gripping the fabric of her blouse.

"You think you're so smart," he said, his breath hot against her ear. "You think you're better than me. Let's see how smart you feel after this."

The push came without warning. One moment Sharifa was standing at the bottom of the stairs, and the next she was falling backward, Avinash's hands propelling her upward with vicious force. She tried to catch herself, hands scrambling for the banister, but her momentum was too great.

Her back hit the stairs with brutal impact, driving what little air remained from her lungs. The wooden edges caught her spine, her shoulders, the back of her head. She tumbled upward in a grotesque reversal of gravity, each step delivering its own sharp punishment.

When she finally stopped, about halfway up the staircase, Sharifa lay still for several seconds, trying to assess the damage. Everything hurt—her back, her head, her already injured ribs. But worse than the physical pain was the realization of how far Avinash had gone this time. He had deliberately tried to seriously hurt her, had used the stairs as a weapon.

"Get up," his voice called from below, but it sounded distant and muffled. "Stop being dramatic. You're fine."

But Sharifa wasn't fine. When she tried to sit up, the room spun violently and nausea crashed over her in waves. She could taste blood in her mouth, could feel it trickling from her nose. Her left shoulder felt wrong, disconnected somehow.

"I said get up!" Avinash was climbing the stairs now, his footsteps heavy with purpose. "You think I'm going to fall for this act? You think you can make me feel guilty with your theatrics?"

Sharifa managed to roll onto her side, though the movement sent fresh waves of pain through her battered body. She could see Avinash approaching, his face twisted with an rage she no longer recognized. This wasn't her husband anymore; this was a stranger who wanted to hurt her.

"Look what you made me do," he said when he reached her. "Look at the mess you've caused. Now I'm going to be late for work because of your drama."

Through the pain and fear, a moment of clarity cut through Sharifa's confusion. This had to stop. Not just this fight, but all of it. The years of escalating violence, the terror that had replaced love, the poisonous atmosphere that was destroying her daughters' childhood. Something had to change, or the next fall down the stairs might be the last thing she ever experienced.

"I'm calling the police," she whispered, the words scraping against her injured throat.

Avinash's expression shifted from anger to something like surprise. "What did you say?"

"I'm calling the police," Sharifa repeated, louder this time despite the pain it caused. "This is over. No more."

For a moment, husband and wife stared at each other across the wreckage of their marriage. Then Avinash's face hardened again, and he took another step toward her.

"You wouldn't dare," he said. "You need me. You can't survive without me, and you know it."

But something had broken inside Sharifa when she hit those stairs—not just physically, but spiritually. The fear that had controlled her for so long was still there, but it was joined now by something stronger: the absolute certainty that she would rather die than live like this for one more day.

"Watch me," she said.

When Avinash reached for her again, Sharifa screamed—a sound of pure terror and rage that she had never heard from her own throat. The sound seemed to shock him into stillness, and in that moment of hesitation, she found the strength to crawl past him toward the phone in the hallway.

Her hands shook as she dialed 911, her vision blurring from the head injury. But when the operator answered, Sharifa's voice was surprisingly steady.

"I need help," she said. "My husband just pushed me down the stairs. I think I need an ambulance."

Behind her, she could hear Avinash's sharp intake of breath, could feel his shock at her betrayal of their conspiracy of silence. For fifteen years, she had protected his reputation, had covered for his violence, had helped maintain the fiction that they were a normal, happy family.

Not anymore.

"Ma'am, are you safe right now?" the operator asked. "Is your husband still in the house?"

Sharifa looked over her shoulder at Avinash, who stood frozen on the stairs, his face cycling through disbelief, rage, and something that might have been fear.

"I will be," she said. "I'm going to be safe now."

The operator's voice was calm and professional. "Police and paramedics are on their way. Can you stay on the line with me?"

"Yes," Sharifa said, never taking her eyes off Avinash.

For several minutes, they remained in tableau—Sharifa on the floor with the phone pressed to her ear, Avinash standing motionless on the stairs. Then, as if waking from a trance, he began moving toward the front door.

"Where are you going?" the operator asked, apparently hearing his footsteps.

"He's leaving," Sharifa said.

"Don't follow him. Wait for the officers to arrive."

Sharifa almost laughed at the suggestion. Following Avinash was the last thing she would ever do again. She was done following, done accommodating, done protecting the man who had tried to kill her on their staircase.

The sound of sirens grew louder, and within minutes, paramedics were examining her injuries while police officers took her statement. Avinash was nowhere to be found—he had disappeared into the morning, leaving behind only the evidence of his violence and the wreckage of their marriage.

"You're going to need X-rays," the paramedic said, gently probing her ribs. "Possible concussion too. We should get you to the hospital."

"My daughters," Sharifa said suddenly. "They'll be coming home from school."

"Do you have someone who can pick them up?" Officer Martinez asked. "Someone they can stay with tonight?"

Sharifa thought of Mrs. Kowalski, who had probably heard everything and would understand without needing explanations. "Yes," she said. "I have someone."

As they loaded her into the ambulance, Sharifa caught sight of herself in the rearview mirror. Her face was swollen, her hair disheveled, her clothes torn and bloody. She looked like exactly what she was—a woman who had survived attempted murder.

But she had survived. And for the first time in years, Sharifa felt something she had almost forgotten: hope.

Chapter 11
New Rules

The hospital discharge papers felt like a declaration of independence in Sharifa's hands. Three cracked ribs, a mild concussion, and enough bruises to paint a roadmap of violence—but she was alive, and more importantly, she was awake. For the first time in years, she could see her situation clearly, without the fog of fear and manipulation that had clouded her judgment.

"Mrs. Sharma," Officer Martinez said, settling into the chair beside her hospital bed. "We've been looking for your husband since yesterday, but he hasn't returned to the house. Do you have any idea where he might be?"

"Probably with one of his women," Sharifa said matter-of-factly, surprised by how steady her own voice sounded. "He has several he rotates between."

The officer raised an eyebrow but didn't comment on the casual way she'd mentioned her husband's infidelity. "We need to discuss your options. You can file charges for domestic assault, and given the severity of your injuries, it would likely result in serious consequences for him."

Sharifa stared out the hospital window at the parking lot below, watching people come and go with their ordinary problems and normal lives. "What happens to my daughters if their father goes to prison?"

"They would remain with you, of course. And there are resources available—shelters, counseling services, financial assistance programs."

"I don't need financial assistance," Sharifa said quietly. "I have a good job, savings. What I need is for him to understand that things have changed forever."

Officer Martinez leaned forward. "Mrs. Sharma, I've seen cases like this before. Often, when the abuser realizes they've lost control, the violence escalates. Your husband crossed a line yesterday—he could have killed you on those stairs."

"Yes," Sharifa agreed. "He could have. But he didn't. And that's the last time he'll ever get the chance."

Two days later, Sharifa returned home to find Avinash waiting for her. He was sitting at the kitchen table, unshaven and hollow-eyed, his hands wrapped around a cup of coffee that had long since gone cold. When she walked through the door with Mrs. Kowalski supporting her arm, he looked up with an expression she had never seen before—genuine fear.

"Sharifa," he said, starting to rise from his chair.

"Sit down," she said, her voice carrying an authority that surprised them both. "We need to talk."

The girls rushed to greet her, their faces bright with relief. They had been staying with Mrs. Kowalski since the incident, and Sharifa could see they'd been well cared for but worried.

"Mama, are you okay?" Saira asked, her eyes taking in the visible bruises on Sharifa's face and arms.

"I'm going to be fine, beta," Sharifa said, hugging them both carefully. "But things are going to be different now."

"Different how?" Priya wanted to know.

Sharifa looked at Avinash over her daughters' heads. "Your father and I need to have a private conversation. Why don't you go upstairs and unpack your things?"

When the girls had reluctantly obeyed, Sharifa turned her full attention to her husband. Up close, she could see he'd been drinking, but he wasn't drunk—just desperate and afraid.

"The police are looking for you," she said.

"I know." His voice was barely a whisper. "Sharifa, I'm so sorry. I never meant for things to go so far."

"But they did go that far. And they would have gone further if I hadn't called for help."

"It won't happen again," he said quickly. "I swear to you, on my mother's grave, it will never happen again."

Sharifa studied his face, noting the genuine distress there. For a moment, she almost felt sorry for him—this man who had once been her partner, who had once made her laugh, who had fathered her children. But sympathy was a luxury she could no longer afford.

"You're right," she said. "It won't happen again. Because I'm going to make sure it can't."

"What do you mean?"

Sharifa walked to the kitchen counter and picked up the restraining order paperwork Officer Martinez had given her. "I can file these papers today. One phone call, and you'll be arrested and charged with assault. The girls will lose their father, you'll lose your job, and everyone in our community will know exactly what kind of man you are."

Avinash's face went pale. "You wouldn't—"

"Oh, but I would," Sharifa interrupted. "I should. Any reasonable person would tell me to send you to prison and file for divorce. But I'm not going to do that."

"You're not?"

"No. Because as much as I hate what you've become, the girls still love you. And despite everything, I don't want to destroy their relationship with their father if it can be avoided."

Relief flooded Avinash's features, but Sharifa held up a hand to stop him from speaking.

"However," she continued, "if you want to stay in this house and remain part of this family, things will be done my way. Completely my way. Is that clear?"

"Yes," he said quickly. "Anything you want."

"Here are the rules," Sharifa said, settling into the chair across from him. "Rule number one: You will never raise your voice to me again. Ever. You will never touch me in anger, never threaten me, never intimidate me in any way. The first time you violate this rule will be the last time, because I will call the police immediately."

Avinash nodded eagerly.

"Rule number two: You will have no say in how I raise our daughters. No criticism of my parenting, no undermining my decisions, no attempts to turn them against me. They are my children first, and I will protect them from any negative influence—including you."

"But I'm their father—"

"You forfeited many of your parental rights when you decided to terrorize their mother," Sharifa said coldly. "If you want to rebuild a relationship with them, you'll do it by earning their trust and respect, not by asserting authority you no longer possess."

Avinash's jaw tightened, but he remained silent.

"Rule number three: You will contribute financially to this household, but you will have no control over how that money is spent. I will manage all finances, pay all bills, make all financial decisions. Your paycheck will go into an account I control, and you will receive an allowance for your personal expenses."

"An allowance?" The word came out strangled.

"Like a teenager," Sharifa confirmed. "Because that's how you've been behaving. When you prove you can act like a responsible adult, we can revisit the financial arrangements."

"This is humiliating," Avinash said.

"Not as humiliating as being arrested for domestic violence," Sharifa replied. "Rule number four: You will sleep in the spare room. You will not enter my bedroom without permission. You will not expect any physical intimacy until and unless I decide I want it— which, honestly, may be never."

"Sharifa, please—"

"I'm not finished. Rule number five: You will not drink alcohol in this house. If I smell alcohol on your breath when you come home, you will leave immediately and not return until you're sober."

"You can't control what I do outside this house," Avinash protested.

"You're absolutely right," Sharifa agreed. "I can't and I won't try. What you do with your free time is your business. But what happens in this house is my business, and I will not tolerate any behavior that makes me or the girls uncomfortable."

She leaned forward, her voice becoming steely. "Rule number six, and this is the most important one: You will treat me with respect at all times. You will speak to me politely, you will acknowledge my authority in this household, and you will never again treat me as if I'm your property or your subordinate."

"And if I don't agree to these rules?" Avinash asked quietly.

"Then you pack your bags right now and find somewhere else to live. I'll file the restraining order and the assault charges, and you can explain to everyone why your family fell apart."

The silence stretched between them for several long minutes. Sharifa could hear the girls moving around upstairs, their voices drifting down as they settled back into their rooms. Normal childhood sounds in what was no longer a normal household.

"These rules," Avinash said finally, "how long would they be in effect?"

"Until I decide they're no longer necessary. Which might be years, or might be never. That's entirely up to you and how you choose to behave going forward."

"This isn't a marriage anymore," he said bitterly.

"No," Sharifa agreed. "It's not. What we had is dead, killed by your choices and your violence. This is something else—a practical arrangement that allows our daughters to grow up with both parents in the house while keeping me safe from further harm."

Avinash sat back in his chair, the full weight of his new reality settling over him. "What will people think? How will we explain this to the community?"

"We won't explain anything. What happens in this house is private. But if anyone asks me directly, I will tell them the truth—that you became violent and I had to take steps to protect myself and our children."

"You would ruin my reputation?"

"Your reputation was ruined the moment you pushed me down those stairs," Sharifa said. "I'm just giving you a chance to salvage what's left of your relationship with your daughters."

The conversation was interrupted by the sound of the front door opening. Saira called out, "Mama, Mrs. Kowalski brought your mail!"

"We'll be right there, beta," Sharifa called back. Then, turning to Avinash: "So what's it going to be? Do you accept my terms, or do I make that phone call?"

Avinash stared at the table for a long moment, his hands clenched into fists. When he finally looked up, his eyes were filled with something that might have been hatred, but Sharifa no longer cared what he felt about her.

"I accept," he said through gritted teeth.

"Good. Then we understand each other. Mrs. Kowalski will be staying for dinner tonight to help me get settled back in. Tomorrow, you'll move your things to the spare room, and we'll begin this new arrangement."

"And the girls? What do we tell them?"

"We tell them that Mama and Papa have decided to live differently, but that we both love them very much and nothing will change their relationship with either of us."

"Will you tell them about... what happened?"

Sharifa considered this. "They're old enough to understand that adults sometimes have serious disagreements. They don't need to know the details, but they deserve to know that the fighting is over and that everyone in this house is safe now."

Over the next few weeks, the new dynamic established itself with surprising ease. Avinash moved his belongings to the spare room without complaint, began turning over his paychecks as instructed, and maintained the careful politeness that Sharifa had demanded.

The girls adapted with the resilience of childhood, simply accepting that Papa now slept in the small room down the hall and that the house was quieter than it used to be. If they missed the warmth that had once existed between their parents, they didn't say so—perhaps because they were old enough to remember when that warmth had curdled into something frightening.

"Are you and Papa getting divorced?" Saira asked one evening while helping Sharifa with dishes.

"I don't think so," Sharifa replied honestly. "We're just learning to live together in a different way."

"Like roommates?"

"Something like that."

Priya, ever the observer, seemed to understand the situation more clearly than her older sister. "Papa seems scared now," she said matter-of-factly one morning at breakfast.

"What makes you say that?" Sharifa asked.

"He talks to you like he's afraid you might get angry. Before, you were the one who looked scared."

The child's perception was startling in its accuracy. Sharifa realized that her daughters had been watching and learning from their parents' dynamic all along, absorbing lessons about power and respect that would shape their own future relationships.

"What do you think about that change?" she asked carefully.

Priya considered the question with her characteristic seriousness. "I think it's better when nobody has to be scared."

Months passed, and the arrangement proved more stable than Sharifa had expected. Avinash followed the rules meticulously, perhaps understanding that any violation would result in immediate consequences. He was polite but distant, contributing financially while having no input on how the money was spent, present but marginalized in the daily life of the family.

To outside observers, they probably looked like a family going through a rough patch—not uncommon among couples approaching their twentieth anniversary. The community didn't pry, accepting Sharifa's vague explanations about "working through some challenges" with the diplomatic blindness that immigrant communities often maintained regarding private family matters.

"You seem different," observed Maria from work during one of their lunch conversations. "Stronger somehow."

"I feel different," Sharifa replied. "Like I finally figured out who I am and what I'm willing to accept."

"And Avinash? How is he adjusting to... whatever changes you've made?"

Sharifa smiled. "He's learning to be a better man. Whether he succeeds is entirely up to him."

At home, evenings settled into a new rhythm. Avinash would help the girls with homework when asked, then retreat to his room to read or watch television. Sharifa would handle bedtime routines, household management, and financial planning without interference or criticism.

It wasn't a marriage in any traditional sense, but it was peaceful. And after years of walking on eggshells, peace felt like the greatest luxury imaginable.

"Do you think Papa will ever be the way he used to be?" Saira asked one night as Sharifa tucked her into bed.

"Which way he used to be?" Sharifa asked gently. "The papa from when you were very small, or the papa from more recently?"

"The nice papa. From before he started being angry all the time."

Sharifa smoothed her daughter's hair, choosing her words carefully. "People can change, beta. But they have to want to change, and they have to do the work to become better. All we can do is give Papa the chance to show us who he wants to be."

As she turned off the lights and headed to her own room, Sharifa reflected on how dramatically her life had shifted. Six months ago, she had been a victim, controlled and terrorized by a man who had somehow convinced her she deserved his violence. Now she was the one setting terms, making rules, determining the conditions under which their family would function.

The transformation hadn't happened overnight, and it wasn't complete. Some days she still felt the old fear, still caught herself monitoring Avinash's moods and adjusting her behavior accordingly. But those moments were becoming less frequent, replaced by a calm confidence she had never possessed before.

Standing at her bedroom window, looking out at the quiet street where she had once believed she would live happily ever after, Sharifa allowed herself to feel proud of what she had accomplished. She had survived, she had protected her daughters, and she had found a way to reclaim her power without destroying her children's family entirely.

It wasn't the ending she had dreamed of when she first arrived in America, but it was an ending she could live with. And for the first time in years, that felt like victory enough.

Chapter 12
The Stroke

The call came on a Tuesday morning in October 1987, just as Sharifa was reviewing the monthly accounts receivable reports at her office. She had been promoted again the previous year, now serving as senior credit manager for the firm, and her desk was covered with the kind of complex financial puzzles that she had come to enjoy solving.

"Mrs. Sharma?" The voice on the other end of the line was crisp and professional. "This is Dr. Chen at Queens General Hospital. Your husband has been brought to our emergency department."

Sharifa's pen stopped moving across the spreadsheet. "What happened?"

"He collapsed at his workplace. We believe he's suffered a stroke. Can you come in as soon as possible?"

The word 'stroke' hit her like cold water. Despite everything that had transpired between them over the past four years of their strange new living arrangement, Avinash was still her husband, still the father of her children. And at fifty-two, he was far too young for this kind of medical crisis.

"I'll be there in twenty minutes," she said, already reaching for her purse.

The drive to the hospital was surreal. For four years, she had lived with Avinash under the strict rules she had established after the incident on the stairs. He had followed those rules meticulously, transforming from the violent, controlling man he had become into something quieter, more subdued. They had existed in the same house like polite strangers, sharing space but not intimacy, cooperating in the raising of their daughters but maintaining emotional distance.

Now, suddenly, she was faced with the possibility of losing him entirely, and she was surprised to discover that the prospect brought her no satisfaction.

At the hospital, Dr. Chen explained that Avinash had suffered what appeared to be a moderate stroke affecting the left side of his brain. The good news was that he was conscious and responsive. The concerning news was that it was difficult to determine the full extent of the damage until the swelling in his brain subsided.

"Can I see him?" Sharifa asked.

"Of course. But I should warn you—stroke patients often experience personality changes, at least temporarily. He may seem different from the man you know."

If only you knew, Sharifa thought, following the doctor down the sterile corridor toward the intensive care unit.

Avinash was awake when she entered his room, staring at the ceiling with an expression of confusion that made him look younger than his years. When he turned his head to look at her, she could see that his face was slightly drooped on the right side.

"Sharifa," he said, and she was relieved that his speech, while slurred, was understandable.

"How are you feeling?" she asked, settling into the chair beside his bed.

"Scared," he said simply, and the honesty in his voice was striking. The old Avinash would never have admitted to fear, would never have shown such vulnerability.

"The doctors say you're going to be okay," she said gently. "It will take time to recover, but you're going to be okay."

"I can't move my right arm," he said, tears beginning to form in his eyes. "I can't feel my right leg properly."

"The feeling may come back as you heal. And even if it doesn't, there are therapies that can help you adapt."

They sat in silence for several minutes, the beeping of medical equipment providing a rhythm to their awkward reunion. Finally, Avinash spoke again.

"Will you call the girls? I want to see them."

"Of course. They're at school now, but I'll bring them this evening."

"Sharifa," he said as she started to stand. "I'm sorry. For everything. I know I can't undo what I did, but I'm sorry."

She looked at him for a long moment—this man who had once been her greatest love and her greatest fear, now reduced to a hospital patient dependent on machines and medications. "I know you are," she said finally. "We'll talk about all of that when you're stronger."

The girls took the news of their father's stroke with the seriousness that had characterized their approach to all family crises since the incident four years earlier. At fifteen and thirteen, they were old enough to understand the gravity of the situation but young enough to still need their mother's guidance on how to process it.

"Is he going to die?" Priya asked with characteristic directness.

"The doctors don't think so," Sharifa replied. "But he's going to need help recovering, and he may not be exactly the same as he was before."

"Different how?" Saira wanted to know.

"We'll have to wait and see. Sometimes stroke patients have trouble with speech or memory. Sometimes they need help with basic tasks like walking or feeding themselves."

The implications hung in the air between them. After four years of their father living in the house but playing a minimal role in their daily lives, they were now facing the possibility of him becoming even more dependent.

When they visited him that evening, Avinash's joy at seeing his daughters was palpable. His eyes filled with tears as they approached his bed, and he reached out with his functioning left hand to touch their faces.

"My beautiful girls," he said, his speech still slurred but his meaning clear. "I've missed you."

It was a strange thing to say, given that he had been living in the same house with them for years. But Sharifa understood what he meant—he had missed being truly present in their lives, missed having a real relationship with them rather than the careful, distant politeness that had characterized their interactions since she had established her rules.

"We missed you too, Papa," Saira said, taking his hand. "Are you in pain?"

"Not physical pain," he replied, looking directly at Sharifa. "But other kinds of pain, yes."

Over the next several weeks, as Avinash underwent various therapies and medical evaluations, Sharifa found herself in an unexpected role: advocate and caregiver for the man who had once terrorized her. The irony was not lost on her, but she approached the responsibility with the same methodical competence she brought to everything else in her life.

She arranged for physical therapy sessions, speech therapy consultations, and follow-up appointments with neurologists. She researched stroke recovery techniques and dietary modifications that might aid in his healing. She coordinated with his workplace to ensure his medical leave was properly documented and his benefits remained intact.

"Why are you doing all this?" Avinash asked one afternoon when she arrived at his hospital room with a folder full of insurance paperwork and therapy schedules.

"Because you're still the father of my children," she replied matter-of-factly. "And because it's the right thing to do."

"Even after everything I put you through?"

Sharifa set down the folder and really looked at him. The stroke had left him physically diminished—his right side remained partially paralyzed, and he needed assistance with many basic tasks. But more than that, it seemed to have stripped away the angry, controlling persona he had cultivated during the worst years of their marriage.

"What you did to me was unforgivable," she said carefully. "But that doesn't mean I want to see you suffer needlessly. And our daughters need to see that people can choose to do the right thing even when it's difficult."

"You're a better person than I deserved," he said quietly.

"I'm the person I chose to become," she corrected. "Just like you chose to become the person you were. The difference is, I chose to become someone I could respect."

After three weeks in the hospital, Avinash was discharged home with instructions for continued physical therapy and regular medical follow-ups. Sharifa had spent the time preparing the house for his return, installing safety rails in the bathroom and rearranging furniture to accommodate his limited mobility.

The girls had mixed feelings about their father's homecoming. They were glad he was alive and recovering, but they were also anxious about how his presence would affect the peaceful household dynamic they had grown accustomed to.

"Will he still follow the rules?" Priya asked as they waited for the hospital transport to arrive.

"Modified versions of them," Sharifa replied. "His medical condition changes some things, but the basic principles remain the same. This is still my household, and everyone in it will treat each other with respect."

When Avinash was wheeled into their front hallway, supported by a physical therapist and laden with medical equipment, Sharifa felt a complex mixture of emotions. This broken man bore little resemblance to either version of her husband—not the loving partner from their early years or the violent antagonist from their middle years. This was someone new, someone she would have to learn to understand.

Over the following months, they developed new routines around Avinash's limitations and recovery needs. He required help with bathing and dressing, tasks that Sharifa performed with clinical efficiency rather than intimacy. She prepared special meals that accommodated his dietary restrictions and managed his increasingly complex medication schedule.

"I feel useless," he confided one evening as she helped him into his pajamas.

"You're recovering," she replied. "That's your job right now—to focus on getting stronger."

"I may never be the man I was before."

"Good," Sharifa said without hesitation. "The man you were before nearly destroyed this family. Maybe being a different man will be an improvement."

The conversation seemed to plant a seed in his mind. Over the following weeks, she noticed him making conscious efforts to engage with the girls in ways he never had before—really listening when they talked about school, asking thoughtful questions about their friends and interests, offering gentle encouragement rather than criticism.

"Papa seems nicer now," Saira observed one evening while she and Sharifa prepared dinner together.

"Do you think it's because of the stroke?" Priya added, with her usual directness.

"I think the stroke made him realize how fragile life is," Sharifa replied carefully. "Sometimes it takes a crisis to help people understand what really matters."

What surprised her most was how natural it felt to care for him. Despite all the years of anger and fear, despite the rules and boundaries she had established to protect herself, there was something deeply ingrained in her nature that responded to suffering with compassion. She found herself genuinely hoping for his recovery, genuinely pleased when he showed improvements in his speech or regained some sensation in his right hand.

"You don't have to do this," he said one afternoon as she helped him with his physical therapy exercises.

"I know I don't have to," she replied, guiding his arm through the prescribed range of motion. "I choose to."

"Why?"

Sharifa paused in her movements, considering the question. "Because this is who I am. I take care of people. It's not dependent on whether they deserve it or whether they've earned it. It's just who I am."

The recovery process was slow and sometimes frustrating. Avinash regained most of his speech clarity and some function in his right side, but he continued to need assistance with many daily tasks. More importantly, the stroke seemed to have genuinely altered his personality in ways that went beyond the physical symptoms.

The angry, controlling man who had terrorized his family was gone, replaced by someone quieter, more thoughtful, more grateful for small kindnesses. Whether this change was due to brain damage or genuine personal growth, Sharifa couldn't say. But she found this version of her husband much easier to live with.

"Do you remember," he said one evening as they sat in the living room—he in his recliner, she on the couch with a book—"when we first moved to this house? How excited we were about our future?"

"I remember," Sharifa said, not looking up from her reading.

"I ruined it all, didn't I? I took something beautiful and I destroyed it."

"Yes," she said simply. "You did."

"Do you think... is there any chance we could find our way back to something good? Not what we had before, but something new?"

Sharifa finally looked at him, studying his face for signs of manipulation or false hope. But she saw only genuine regret and a tentative vulnerability that seemed authentic.

"I don't know," she said honestly. "That would depend on whether you're truly different now, or whether you're just different because you're dependent on me."

"How can I prove the difference?"

"Time," she said. "Time will tell us both what kind of man you are now."

As the months passed, Avinash continued to improve physically while seeming to settle into his new role in the family. He was no longer the head of household, no longer the primary decision-maker, but he found ways to contribute that worked within the boundaries Sharifa had established.

He helped the girls with their homework, drawing on his engineering background to assist with their math and science classes. He took over some household tasks that could be performed while seated, like folding laundry and organizing paperwork. He even began cooking simple meals, something he had never done during the earlier years of their marriage.

"You're becoming quite the chef," Sharifa observed one Sunday afternoon, finding him carefully preparing ingredients for soup.

"I have time to learn now," he replied. "And it feels good to contribute something useful."

The dynamic between them was unlike anything they had experienced in their twenty-three years of marriage. It wasn't romantic love—that had been casualties of his violence and her necessary emotional self-protection. But it wasn't the tense coexistence of their post-incident years either. It was something new: a cautious partnership based on mutual respect and shared commitment to their daughters' wellbeing.

"Are you happy?" he asked her one day as she drove him to a medical appointment.

The question caught her off guard. "Happy is a complicated word. I'm content. I'm at peace. I feel safe in my own home. That's more than I had for many years."

"I'm glad," he said quietly. "You deserve to feel safe."

It was perhaps the most important thing he had ever said to her, this acknowledgment that her safety and peace of mind mattered, that they were not negotiable terms in any relationship. Coming from the man who had once threatened both, the words carried particular weight.

As they pulled into the medical center parking lot, Sharifa reflected on the strange journey that had brought them to this point. She was no longer the frightened young woman who had married for practical reasons, nor the terrorized wife who had endured violence for years. She was someone new: a woman who had learned to claim her power and use it wisely, who could show compassion without sacrificing strength.

And Avinash—whether through brain injury or genuine personal growth—had become someone she could tolerate, even occasionally appreciate. It wasn't the marriage she had once dreamed of, but it was a partnership she could live with.

For now, that was enough.

Chapter 13
Freedom

The phone call came at 6:43 on a Wednesday morning in March 1993, the shrill sound cutting through the peaceful silence that had become Sharifa's favorite part of each day. She had been awake for twenty minutes already, sitting at her kitchen table with her first cup of coffee, reviewing her financial records and planning the day ahead—a routine she had developed during the years when control over her own life had seemed impossible.

"Mrs. Sharma?" The voice was professional but gentle. "This is Dr. Patel at Queens General. I'm calling about your husband."

Sharifa set down her coffee cup, her mind immediately calculating the possibilities. Avinash had been having more frequent dizzy spells lately, side effects from his medications that his doctors had been monitoring but hadn't considered serious.

"What's happened?" she asked.

"He was brought in by ambulance about an hour ago. I'm afraid he suffered a massive stroke during the night. We've done everything we can, but he passed away about twenty minutes ago."

The words hung in the air like smoke, taking several seconds to fully register. Avinash was dead. After six years of caring for him following his first stroke, after twenty-eight years of marriage that had encompassed every emotion from love to terror to cautious respect, it was over.

"Mrs. Sharma? Are you there?"

"Yes," she said quietly. "I'm here. What do I need to do?"

The practical questions that followed were familiar territory for Sharifa. She had spent decades managing crises, solving problems, organizing the details of life while others fell apart around her. The administrative requirements of death—paperwork, funeral arrangements, notification of relatives—were just another puzzle to solve.

"I'll be there within the hour," she told Dr. Patel. "Thank you for calling."

She hung up the phone and sat in the morning stillness, waiting for grief to hit her. But instead of sadness, what she felt was something closer to relief. Not relief that Avinash was dead—she had never wished him harm—but relief that the long, complex chapter of their relationship was finally closed.

The girls, now twenty-one and nineteen, took the news with the complicated emotions of children who had loved their father despite understanding his flaws. Saira, now in her senior year of college studying pharmacy, cried quietly but without surprise. Priya, a sophomore majoring in pre-med, asked practical questions about the funeral arrangements and offered to handle the notifications to extended family.

"How are you doing, Mama?" Saira asked as they sat together in the hospital family waiting room, signing forms and collecting Avinash's personal effects.

"I'm okay," Sharifa replied honestly. "I think I said goodbye to the marriage years ago. This is just... the final paperwork."

The funeral was held on a gray Saturday morning at the community center where their Caribbean immigrant community gathered for celebrations and sorrows. The turnout was respectable—work colleagues, neighbors, fellow members of the cricket league Avinash had joined during his recovery years. People offered condolences with the appropriate solemnity, speaking about his engineering skills and his love for his daughters.

What surprised Sharifa was how many people approached her specifically to comment on her devotion during his illness.

"You were such a good wife to him," said Mrs. Singh, who had known them since their early days in Queens. "The way you cared for him after the stroke, helping him through his recovery. Not many women would have been so dedicated."

Sharifa accepted these comments with polite gratitude, knowing that the community saw only the caretaking of the final years, not the violence and terror that had preceded them. She had no interest in explaining the complexity of their relationship to people who preferred simple narratives about marriage and duty.

But it was her own family's reaction that caught her most off guard.

"Why aren't you crying?" Sharifa's younger sister Nishat asked quietly as they stood beside the casket receiving condolences.

"Should I be?" Sharifa replied.

"He was your husband for nearly thirty years. The father of your children. It's... unusual for a widow to be so composed."

Sharifa looked around the room at the gathered mourners, at the displays of flowers and the photographs of Avinash from happier times, at her daughters who were handling their grief with dignity and strength.

"I cried for this marriage years ago," she said finally. "I cried for the man I thought he was, for the life I thought we would have, for the woman I had to become to survive. I have no more tears to shed today."

The comment clearly disturbed some of her relatives, but Sharifa found she didn't care. She had spent too many years managing other people's perceptions, protecting other people's feelings, making herself smaller to accommodate other people's comfort. At fifty-one, she was finally free to be herself without apology.

The months following Avinash's death brought a series of revelations about the life she could now live. The house, which had been purchased jointly but maintained entirely through her financial management, was now solely hers. The insurance payout was substantial—enough to pay off the mortgage completely and still have a significant sum left over. Combined with her retirement savings and the equity she had built over the years, she found herself genuinely financially independent for the first time in her adult life.

More importantly, she was emotionally and psychologically free in ways she hadn't fully appreciated were missing. There was no one to report to, no one whose moods she needed to manage, no one whose approval she needed to seek. She could eat what she wanted, go where she wanted, make decisions based purely on her own preferences and values.

"What will you do now?" asked Mr. Cohen during her retirement party at the office. At fifty-one, she was young to be retiring, but the insurance settlement had made continued work optional rather than necessary.

"Travel," she said immediately. "I want to see the world."

It wasn't something she had ever discussed with anyone, this secret dream that had grown during all those years of careful budgeting and financial planning. But now, with money in the bank and no one to consult but herself, the possibility felt real for the first time.

Within six months of Avinash's death, Sharifa had booked her first solo vacation—two weeks in London, a destination that had fascinated her since her school days in Guyana. She had never traveled alone, had never even made major decisions without considering their impact on other people. The experience was both terrifying and exhilarating.

"Are you sure about this, Mama?" Priya asked as they drove to the airport. "You've never been anywhere by yourself."

"That's exactly why I need to do it," Sharifa replied. "I want to know what it feels like to be completely responsible for my own happiness."

London was a revelation. Walking through Hyde Park at her own pace, choosing restaurants based purely on her curiosity, spending entire afternoons in museums without having to consider anyone else's interests—it was a kind of freedom she hadn't even known she was missing.

She called the girls from her hotel room each evening, describing the sights and experiences of her day, but what she couldn't fully convey was the profound sense of coming alive that the trip gave her. For the first time in decades, she was experiencing life without the filter of other people's needs and demands.

"You sound different," Saira observed during one of these calls. "Happy in a way I don't think I've ever heard before."

"I feel different," Sharifa admitted. "I feel like myself again. Maybe for the first time since I was very young."

The trip to London was followed by others—Paris, Rome, Amsterdam, Madrid. Sharifa discovered that she was a natural traveler, adaptable and curious and unintimidated by foreign languages or customs. She began learning French through audio tapes, picked up basic Italian from phrase books, navigated subway systems and currency exchanges with the same methodical competence she had once brought to managing household finances.

More importantly, she discovered that she genuinely enjoyed her own company. All those years of believing she needed someone else to make her life complete had been a lie she had told herself out of fear and conditioning. Traveling alone, she found herself more open to new experiences, more willing to strike up conversations with strangers, more present in each moment without the distraction of managing someone else's needs.

"I've been to fifteen countries now," she told Mrs. Kowalski during one of their over-the-fence conversations. "Next month I'm going to Greece."

"Aren't you lonely?" Mrs. Kowalski asked. "All that traveling by yourself?"

"Not lonely," Sharifa replied. "Free."

The distinction was important. Loneliness was something she had experienced regularly during her marriage, surrounded by people but unable to be authentically herself. Solitude, by contrast, was a choice that allowed her to reconnect with parts of herself that had been suppressed for years.

As the months turned into years, Sharifa settled into a routine that balanced her love of travel with her desire to maintain close relationships with her daughters and enjoy her comfortable home. She would take three or four major trips annually, spending weeks exploring new countries and cultures, then return to Queens to tend her garden, visit with friends, and catch up on her daughters' lives.

Saira graduated from pharmacy school and found a position at a major hospital, specializing in medication management for elderly patients. Priya was accepted to medical school and had decided to pursue a career in family medicine, inspired partly by watching her father's recovery from his first stroke.

"Are you proud of us?" Priya asked during one of their regular Sunday dinners.

"Beyond proud," Sharifa replied. "You both became the strong, independent women I hoped you would be."

"We learned from you," Saira said. "Watching how you handled everything with Papa, how you took care of yourself and us even when things were terrible—that taught us that women can be strong and kind at the same time."

The observation meant more to Sharifa than any compliment she had ever received. Despite all her mistakes, despite the years when she had felt powerless and afraid, she had somehow managed to model strength and resilience for her daughters.

By her sixtieth birthday in 2002, Sharifa had traveled to forty-three countries. She had seen the Northern Lights in Norway, walked the Great Wall of China, toured vineyards in Tuscany, watched sunrise over Angkor Wat. Each journey had added layers to her understanding of herself and the world, had reinforced her sense of her own capability and independence.

The celebration dinner her daughters organized for her sixtieth was held at a restaurant that specialized in international cuisine—a fitting choice for a woman who had spent the past decade exploring global cultures.

"What do you want to do for the next decade?" Saira asked as they raised glasses of champagne in toast.

"Everything," Sharifa replied without hesitation. "I want to see everything, experience everything I missed during all those years when I thought my life was defined by other people's needs."

"Any regrets?" Priya asked gently.

Sharifa considered the question seriously. "I regret the years I spent being afraid. I regret not understanding sooner that I had choices, that I didn't have to accept treatment that diminished me. But I don't regret the journey that brought me here."

"Not even Papa?" Saira asked.

"Your father gave me you two," Sharifa replied. "And eventually, our marriage taught me that I was stronger than I ever knew. Those are not small gifts, even if they came at a high price."

As the evening wound down and they prepared to leave the restaurant, Sharifa caught her reflection in the window glass—a woman in her sixties, gray-haired but vibrant, surrounded by successful daughters who respected and loved her. She barely resembled the frightened young woman who had arrived in America forty years earlier, or the battered wife who had called the police that morning in 1983.

She had become someone she could respect, someone she genuinely enjoyed being. And for the first time in her life, that felt like enough.

Walking to the parking lot with her daughters, discussing plans for her upcoming trip to Argentina, Sharifa felt a profound sense of completion. Not the completion of a life ending, but the completion of a transformation that had taken decades to achieve.

She was sixty years old, financially secure, physically healthy, and completely free to design her remaining years according to her own values and desires. She had raised two remarkable daughters, survived a marriage that had nearly destroyed her, and discovered that she was capable of finding joy in her own company.

The young woman who had married for practical reasons, who had endured years of violence out of fear and false obligation, who had once believed she needed someone else's permission to live authentically—that woman was gone. In her place was someone who understood that true freedom came not from the absence of responsibility, but from the ability to choose which responsibilities to accept and which to refuse.

Standing under the streetlight beside her car, hugging her daughters goodbye before driving home to her quiet house and her comfortable bed, Sharifa allowed herself a moment of pure gratitude. She had survived everything life had thrown at her, and she had emerged not just intact but genuinely happy.

Tomorrow she would wake up in her own house, drink coffee at her own pace, and make plans that pleased no one but herself. And the day after that, and the day after that, for as many days as she had left.

It was, she realized, exactly the life she had always deserved.